NEW ... ...ST!

Spur got ... ...el from where it had ... ... of the Conestoga box ... ...y use.

He showed it to the women.

"Do you know what this is for?" he shouted. Before they could answer, he dug a spadeful of earth and flung it away from them.

"This is a shovel, and if you insist on making the trip against my recommendation and against that of Major Donaldson of the United States Army, then this shovel will be used often to bury our dead before we get to Roswell!"

Spur marched back to the wagon, secured the shovel where it had been before and walked to his bay. He mounted and glared at both women. Both returned his stare calmly.

"We continue," Mother Superior said.

"We continue," Chiquita echoed.

The middle-aged nun on the wagon seat briskly slapped the reins on the mules' backs and the Conestoga rolled forward. Chiquita, smiling at Spur, swung her horse around and moved in front of the wagon, taking the lead.

Spur McCoy, mother hen to eight little chicks and one dragon, scowled and watched the wagon moving westward.

When it was about fifty yards away, he took off his hat, wiped the sweat from his forehead, then reset the low crowned Stetson and, still scowling, rode after them.

Also in the *Spur* Series:

SPUR #14

SAVAGE SISTERS

DIRK FLETCHER

LEISURE BOOKS NEW YORK CITY

A LEISURE BOOK®

July 2004

Published by

Dorchester Publishing Co., Inc.
200 Madison Avenue
New York, NY 10016

ISBN 0-8439-2325-3

Printed in the United States of America.

Visit us on the web at www.dorchesterpub.com.

ONE

Spur McCoy lay back on the soft bed in the Hotel Texas and relaxed, an unopened telegram in his hand. He'd been on a jolting, bouncing, hard-seated stagecoach for the last five days getting to Lubbock, Texas and now he was going to take it easy for a few hours. The matchbox sized room was not the fanciest he had ever seen—maybe eight by ten feet with a bed, one chair, a washstand with the usual heavy porcelain bowl and rose painted porcelain pitcher full of water. The dresser had two drawers and a wavy mirror. A kerosene lamp sat on top and a packet of *stinker* matches lay close at hand.

The walls were painted plaster over lath. He could tell by the uneven surface. One of the walls had been covered with flowered wallpaper to brighten up the room. It would have helped if the pattern had matched from one section to the other. It wasn't a palace, but it was home for a couple of days.

McCoy was a big man at six-two and two

hundred pounds. He was tanned a light brown and his windblown brown hair had a reddish cast in certain lights. Mutton chop sideburns met his full, reddish moustache. He stared at the world from slightly jaded green eyes that had seen more than their share of outlaws, raiders and killers.

Now he looked at the telegram again and put it down. No sense in reading it until after supper. It was his new assignment and he wanted to put off knowing what it was for a while. He had hit town on the noon stage, had an hour long bath and then taken a nap on a real bed with springs! Now he should be getting dressed for supper.

Yes! He would dress up for supper. It had been a long time since he had even thought of wearing a tie. It would be more like the family suppers back in the New York City townhouse. That was longer ago than he cared to think about. But he would dress.

Lubbock, Texas was one hell of a long way from New York, and the rich, plush life he had left. But working in the big city business world of his father had not appealed to him.

He sat up and stared at the telegram still sealed in the envelope.

He should open it. The general said his assignment details would be waiting for him when he got to Lubbock. He swung his feet off the bed and dressed. The dark blue suit seemed right. Spur slipped into the pants, tucked in the tails of the ruffled front white shirt and added a black half-inch wide string tie. His belt notched in one hole tighter than usual. Too many days rattling around the prairie and deserts without enough to eat. He needed some good home cooking for a change.

Spur pulled on his suit coat and decided not to wear a vest. It felt good to get in his best suit, for a change. He had heard something about an acting troupe in town. Maybe he could catch their show tonight.

orders . . . assignment . . . damn . . .

The yellow envelope lay there on the bed mocking him. He picked it up and tore it open. The yellow sheet fell out, he unfolded it and read:

SPUR McCOY:
HOTEL TEXAS
LUBBOCK, TEXAS

    MEET ON JUNE 28 AT TEXAS RANCH HOUSE HOTEL IN LUB-BOCK WITH MOTHER SUPERIOR M. BENEDICT AND FATHER CLARK. YOU WILL GUIDE AND SHEPHERD THEM AND SIX NUNS, A COVERED WAGON AND VARIOUS RELIGIOUS GOODS, FROM LUBBOCK TO DEVIL WELLS, NEW MEXICO. THE TOWN IS ON THE RIO GRANDE ABOUT 140 MILES SOUTH OF SANTA FE. PICK UP TEN MAN ARMY ESCORT AT CAMP HOUSTON NEAR LUBBOCK. THEY HAVE BEEN NOTIFIED. RE-PORT BY QUICKEST MEANS WHEN ASSIGNMENT COMPLETED.

It was signed by General Wilton D. Halleck, Capitol Investigations, Washington, D.C.

Spur tossed the message on the bed and

snorted. He had to nursemaid seven nuns and a priest through some of the toughest, most hostile, most unforgiving country in the nation? And the damned Apaches were probably prowling again. Mescaleros over this far. Damn, he had tangled with them enough to last a lifetime! The Mescaleros were cunning, crafty and treacherous. They were warriors, looters and killers just for the pure hell of it!

He read the message again. Spur had no idea where it had been sent. There was no telegraph in Lubbock. It had come to the hotel several days ago on one of the regular runs in the stagecoach mail sack, the hotel clerk told him.

Devil Wells! That sounded about right. Somewhere in the middle of the desert, he expected. Seven women! Seven nuns and a priest! Just dandy!

At least he could have a drink before dinner. He found a small bar attached to the hotel and went in for a straight whiskey. He felt it burn all the way to his belly. This was not starting out to be a good evening.

He checked with the barkeep about the actors. He said the traveling troupe of thespians was in town and putting on the last performance that evening in the Lubbock Town Hall. Spur considered ordering another drink. He hadn't seen any good theatre for two years. He would go, alone or with someone, it didn't matter. Then maybe he would get a bottle of the best booze he could find and really tie one on before he met his religious charges.

He looked at the telegram again. Hell, it said June 28 he had to meet them. That was tomorrow! Not even time enough for a three day drunk. At least he could have dinner. He'd decide about the bottle later.

Hotel Texas had a good dining room. Many of the customers were from the town, not travelers. That was always a good sign of fine food. Maybe he could enjoy a delicious meal before he had to make any decisions.

The dining room along the main street side of the hotel was packed. Spur could not see a single free table. A waiter came forward and smiled.

"Sorry, we're a little bit busy right now." He paused, then looked at the far window. "But I see someone leaving. I'll have a table for two in just a moment." The young man hurried away and cleared the table then came back for Spur.

"Yes, right this way." He gave Spur the small, well printed menu. "Oh, since we're so full, would you mind sharing a table if another single person comes in?"

Spur lifted his brows, then smiled. "Only if the person is an attractive young lady."

The waiter grinned and moved away.

McCoy was surprised at the menu. It was quite good, with more than a dozen entrees and numerous side dishes. He felt the hand of an Eastern style management running the dining room. Before he had selected his choice for dinner, someone stopped near his table.

"Begging your pardon sir."

Spur looked up. It was the waiter and someone behind him.

"Sir, you said you would be willing to share your table?"

He stepped aside and the woman behind him

was young, attractive and smiling. She had startling blue eyes and soft, short blonde hair.

Spur stood quickly, grinning.

"Of course, any time. Miss, you're more than welcome. I haven't even ordered yet. Please, may I help you sit down?"

She smiled, her blue pools of eyes dancing.

"You sure you're not waiting for someone? I don't want to impose . . ."

"No, I'm quite alone. I hate to eat by myself. Please, sit down."

She closed her eyes and gave the hint of a nod, then slid gracefully into the chair he held and edged forward to the small table complete with place settings and a white linen tablecloth.

He sat across from her.

"Now, this is a pleasant surprise. My name is Spur McCoy."

She held out her small, white hand that had carefully cared-for nails. "I'm Teresa White. How do you do?"

He took her hand and she shook it strongly then let go.

The waiter opened a white linen napkin and laid it in her lap, then handed her a menu.

"Thank you," she said to the happy waiter.

There was an awkward pause.

Spur cleared his throat and she looked up at him. "I'm delighted you came. Eating alone in a strange town is always a little sad, lonely."

Teresa smiled, then read the menu and her eyes widened.

"Oh! There are so many choices! And all the dishes sound so delicious."

Spur felt himself relaxing. They talked about

the various entrees, and at last he selected the pound and a half steak and she had roast beef with horseradish. As they waited for the meal the waiter brought hot black coffee.

For the first time, Spur noticed that her face seemed softly white, not tanned and brownish like so many frontier women.

"I'm just passing through Lubbock," Spur said. "Are you a resident here?"

She shook her head. "No, some friends and I are going through as well. We'll leave in a day or two."

As the meal ended Spur could not remember what they had talked about. He did remember she had seemed better educated than most women he met on the job. She could play the piano and organ, and originally came from New Orleans.

When they stood, McCoy touched her arm. "There is a troupe of actors in town and I hear they are going to do some Shakespeare. Would you like to go see them with me?"

She hesitated. "No, I couldn't, I . . ." She turned away and he saw confusion on her pretty face. She turned back a moment later. "Well, I love Shakespeare and there are so few chances to see any. I would love to go, but I must get back to my hotel right after the performance."

He frowned.

"Goodness, I hope you don't think I'm being too forward," Teresa said.

"Not at all, no. I see no reason a woman can't do something she wants to. It will be my pleasure to be your escort."

He paid the bill and they walked to the desk.

The clerk told them where the performance was, two blocks down.

"Let's walk," she said.

The traveling troupe was about as Spur had expected. An older man and a woman he guessed was the actor's wife, and a younger man and woman made up the cast. They did scenes from Hamlet, Romeo and Juliet, and Henry the Fifth.

"Just average," Spur whispered during the intermission.

"No, I think they are quite good," Teresa said. "Especially the young Hamlet. He was convincing."

Then it was over and they moved slowly back toward the hotel. She held his arm as they made their way along the boardwalk and across the dust filled streets and soon they were on the second floor of Spur's hotel.

"Oh, I'm sorry," Teresa said. "I wasn't watching where we were. This isn't my hotel."

"You didn't say where you lived. My room is just down the hall. Would you like to stop by for a sip or two of wine?"

"Oh, no, I couldn't," she said quickly, looking up at him with surprise but no real alarm.

He kept walking. At his door he held her arm. "One small glass of wine and I'll rush you back to your hotel. It would be the culmination of a perfect evening with a beautiful lady."

Her smile came slowly, then blossomed. "Well, I don't see what it would hurt. It will round out a simply wonderful evening for me."

Spur unlocked the door and waved her inside. He left the door open a foot and went to the dresser where he had put the bottle of light port —for emergencies. He uncorked it and found two glasses on the washstand.

"Just a little," Teresa said.

He poured each glass half full and handed her one.

"It's a very light port," Spur said. "How do you like it?"

She sipped it, then again. She took a deep breath and her tongue wet her lips. "Yes. Yes, it is good!" She drank again and smiled. "Oh, my! That makes me feel just warm all over!" She sat down suddenly on the bed. "And a little light headed."

Spur sat beside her on the bed. "Are you all right?"

Teresa looked at him, her eyes soft and dreamy. "Oh, yes! I feel fine. It's just . . ." She handed him the glass, closed her eyes and slumped backwards on the bed.

Spur put both glasses on the floor and leaned over her.

"Teresa! Are you not feeling well?"

She smiled but did not open her eyes.

"Feel fine. Just a little warm . . . and, and wondering."

"Would a cold cloth on your forehead help?"

"No." She opened her eyes, caught his hand and kissed it. Then Teresa reached her hand behind his neck and pulled his face down to hers. She kissed him softly, then once again with more force. All at once she scooted away from him and stood up.

"I really do have to go. Mother would kill me if she knew."

Spur stood beside her.

"Do you actually have to go?" He bent and kissed her lips and then the side of her neck and the tip of her ear.

Her arms slid upward and around his neck.

"Spur McCoy, you don't know what that does to me. I absolutely forbid you to kiss me that way again!" But her words came softly and with a longing Spur had not heard in years.

She pulled his head down and he kissed her again. This time her mouth came open for his tongue and he probed deeply, drawing soft moans of pleasure from her. She pushed her hips hard against his, then her breasts pressed firmly to his chest and she held him tightly.

"Darling, marvelous Spur!" she said when their lips parted. "I must leave right now. You know that. I told you that. I can't let you do this to me." But she never let go of him. Her hips began a gentle grinding against his groin and Spur's crotch bulged with his instant erection. She nestled her head against his chest for a moment, then looked up at him, soft blue eyes wanting him.

"Kiss me again before I explode!" she said her voice ragged and breaking with the intensity of her desire.

He kissed her and this time her tongue dug into his open mouth, searching, battling with his tongue and her hips began a slow thrusting and pounding against his now obvious erection.

Spur picked her up and laid her on the bed. She wore a white blouse and light jacket, with a green skirt that brushed the floor. He leaned over looking down at her a moment, then moved to the door and closed it softly, locking it. He turned the key halfway in the lock so no other key could be used. Spur put the straight backed chair under the handle and braced on its rear feet to prevent a forced entry.

Back at the bed she watched him. She pushed the light jacket down her arms and took it off, then lay back on the quilts. Gently he kissed her again and her whole body curled toward him.

She held out her arms and he lay gently on top of her. His hard body crushed her into the mattress and she moaned again with pleasure. Teresa kissed him, then caught his hand and put it over one of her breasts. His hand lay there a moment, feeling the heat of her mound coming through the fabric, then he began soft circular motions and she gasped and smiled.

"Oh, yes, marvelous Spur! Never stop touching me there! Just so wonderful."

He kissed her again, then pushed off her and lifted her up so she sat beside him. Now her breasts pressed against the white blouse and he continued to fondle first one, then both.

He kissed her once more and she nibbled at his lips.

"Teresa. We can stop this any time you want to. If you say the word we will stand up right now and I'll walk you to your hotel . . ."

She smiled and kissed him, then her hand reached out and rubbed the long lump behind his pants fly.

"Wonderful Spur McCoy, it's all right. I'm here because I want to be here. It has been so long. Oh, God, it's been four years! You try to get away now after getting me so worked up this way, and I'll probably shoot you!"

He laughed and she began unbuttoning her blouse. The fasteners went to her chin. He helped and when he was halfway down, his hand slid inside the fabric and found more cloth over her breasts. He caught her mounds and teased her growing, throbbing nipples.

Quickly now she stripped out of the blouse and pulled a chemise off over her head.

Her big breasts swung out, pure white mounds with large pink areolas and her dark nipples throbbing and swolen to a half inch long.

He touched her breasts and she sighed, closed her eyes and reached for his crotch.

"Spur McCoy, I want you! I want you right now!"

TWO

Teresa remained sitting up as Spur lowered his head and kissed her breasts. She squealed in delight and erupted into a long climax that dropped her flat on the bed, her hips slamming upward in a series of jolts and her whole body shaking and vibrating as the tremors shook her again and again.

Spur had moved with her, his mouth covering one breast, chewing on the morsel, sucking the nipple until she at last gave a long sigh and leaned up on her elbows so she could see his mouth on her tit.

"Ooooooh, but that was beautiful, Spur McCoy! I've never been started out that way before. Such a monstrous feeling! So sharp and hard and . . . and wonderful."

"Oh, God!" she said almost as soon as she stopped talking. It was a cry of pain and anger and remorse. She pushed him away and sat at the end of the bed, her head down, her hands clasped in front of her. Teresa still wore her clothing from the waist down. Quiet sobs shook

17

her body now and she turned to him, tears still coming down her cheeks, her eyes red and swollen, nose running.

"Spur McCoy, do you have a cigarette?"

"You smoke?" he asked, surprised. He did not know a woman who smoked in public. He had watched one or two who tried to smoke in private and gave it up. He shook his shirt pocket and came up with a long thin cheroot. The thin, black cigar had been bent in the wrestling match on the bed. He found a match, lit the thin cigar for her and passed it over.

"Never tried a cigar before," she said. "Are they strong?"

Spur said they were.

She puffed on it, then tried to inhale and went into a spate of coughing. She puffed it without inhaling and handed it back to him.

"Thanks. Now for some more of that wine."

They had more port, then she began undressing him. When she had him bare to the waist she played with the hair on his chest, then kissed his nipples, and looked up at him.

"Is that any good? Does it excite you at all?"

"No, it's not something I'm used to."

She rubbed the erection inside his pants.

"But you like that?"

McCoy nodded and stroked her breasts.

"Why does a woman keep her most beautiful part covered up and hidden away?"

"The customs of the people. In Africa breasts are not covered."

"I'm moving down there," Spur said.

She hit him on the shoulder. "Not before you finish the work you've started here."

She stood, and put his hands on her skirt. Spur lifted her back on the bed and hovered over her. He kissed both her breasts, then her mouth and rolled her on top of him. Slowly he pulled her up until her hanging twins dangled over his face.

"I want you really ready before we take off the rest of our clothes." He let her downward until her breasts lowered into his open mouth.

"Yes, yes! You know just what to do!" She purred.

He chewed each tit thoroughly then rolled again until he was on top of her.

Teresa panted now, her eyes wide, her skin flushed. He could feel the raw heat of her desire burning through her thighs against his. He ran his hand down her skirt, found his way under it and came up her leg.

She gasped, then stared at him for several seconds. At last she nodded and lay back, her mouth open, her eyes closed.

Quickly Spur unhooked the skirt and petti-coats and took them off. He started to pull down the knee length panty drawers as well, but her hands held the top of the soft white fabric of the drawers.

He kissed her hands away, then the hot string of kisses continued down from her waist as he pulled the cloth lower and lower.

She gasped again as his lips touched the top of her pubic hair.

As he worked down through the soft blonde crotch growth her hips heaved and Teresa shivered.

"Oh, yes! Oh, yes! Oh, yes!" she whispered to

herself. Her hands rubbed her breasts now, massaging them tenderly, her eyes closed, and she breathed like a blow torch through her mouth.

When Spur came to the soft pink lips he found them swollen, moist. He kissed them and she climaxed. A long low wail came from her mouth and he kissed the soft wetness again. It brought another racking series of spasms as she bounced and jolted and rolled half over before the tremors worked through her.

She lifted up, her eyes half closed, rapture on her face.

"Your turn, your turn," she said and crawled toward him on hands and knees. Eagerly she pulled off his pants and underwear, then sat there staring in amazement at his erection.

"So beautiful!" she shrilled. "Just absolutely wonderful!" She caught his phallus and stroked it, played with his heavy, hairy scrotum, then bent and kissed the purple head.

She kissed it again, then slowly her lips parted, she bent forward and sucked him into her mouth. She pulled half his long shaft down her throat, then began bouncing up and down on it.

Spur caught her shoulders and pushed her away.

"Teresa, that is fantastic, but not for the first time; later." He pushed her down on the bed and hovered over her.

"Yes, Spur McCoy, I want you inside me, right now. Do it before I go out of my mind! Please, now!"

She spread her legs, lifted her knees and Spur went between them, lowered and found the wetness. The natural lubricant lathered him as he drove into her in one strong surge and she squealed in delight.

They made it last for nearly an hour. Each time Spur surged toward his climax, she stopped him, kissed his cheek and began talking.

"Then there was this time in New Orleans when I was just three. My daddy came home and said he lost his job and we were going to have to move. So we moved in with our in-laws, my uncle. He was my dad's brother. It was just a three room house, and the six kids slept in one bedroom and the front room. The adults slept in the other bedrooms.

"They had a big double bed and the first night Dad and his brother decided they might as well share, so they swapped sides of the bed and made love with the other guy's wife. That lasted for about two months, then the women put their feet down and said no more, and so we moved again. Can you imagine that, everybody doing it with everybody else whenever they wanted to? The men loved it, but the women got worried about getting pregnant again."

When she stopped talking Spur lifted her legs to his shoulders and jolted into her. The new angle brought results quickly and he raced to a climax, just as Teresa exploded again and they nearly rolled off the bed before they both collapsed in a heavy sweat on the bed.

Somebody next door pounded the wall.

Teresa laughed.

Spur grinned. "Guess we should be a little more quiet next time."

She looked at him. "Next time?"

"Didn't your first lover tell you that once is never enough?"

Teresa giggled, stroked his chest, then pushed him off her and they lay side by side. "If he ever told me I was too excited to hear him. I was fifteen at the time. Had my tits full grown by then, and all the boys were playing *grab-tit* with me every chance they got. That first time when I lost my virginity was in a garden swing at my other uncle's house. I stayed with his wife while he was on a business trip to Atlanta."

Spur rolled out of bed and got the wine bottle and the two glasses.

They talked and drank wine until the bottle was empty, and made love twice again.

When Spur woke up the next time, it was daylight, and Teresa White had dressed and left. He had no idea when.

McCoy rinsed the old wine taste from his mouth, shaved and got dressed. It was a little after seven A.M. His meeting with the nuns was not until eight.

He had breakfast, walked around two blocks of Lubbock and decided they would be able to find the supplies they needed in town for the trip across the plains and desert to the Rio Grande. If they went. He hoped to talk the priest out of this journey. If they only had ten soldiers as a military escort, it would be a dangerous situation.

At five minutes to eight he walked up the steps to the Texas Ranch House Hotel, and asked the room clerk where he could find Mother Superior Benedict.

The clerk had on heavy glasses and a bow tie. He squinted through the spectacles and pointed.

"Right over there by the front window with the priest. Can't miss them."

Spur looked the way the man pointed. A nun wearing a wimple and long flowing black robes that brushed the floor stood looking out the window. Beside her slouched a slender, short man with thinning brown hair on a high forehead and a priest's white collar. It was time.

Spur walked up to the pair and held out his hand to the priest.

"Father Clark? My name is Spur McCoy."

The priest looked at him curiously for a moment, then a faint smile showed on his sallow face. He sniffed.

"Yes, Mr. McCoy, our guide and protector," the priest said taking the hand limply.

The nun turned and Spur saw the large white collar, the tight white front of the wimple that covered her hair and half her forehead revealing only a round, slightly tanned face with snapping brown eyes, a general nose and a no-nonsense set to her thin mouth.

"Mr. McCoy!" she said, the tone of her voice at once pleasant, friendly and neighborly. Here was a woman who insisted with two words that it would be hard to dislike her.

"We had hoped you would arrive on time from wherever you were. But enough of that, you're here now and we can get down to business." She paused and looked at him.

"Yes, you are certainly big enough for the job. I also would say that you know your way around this part of the country, spend most of your time under the sun and the stars rather than a roof, and that you can use your pistol in that tied down holster."

Father Clark coughed, then wheezed. Spur looked back at him and saw the priest's hands shaking. The churchman scratched his face, and Spur made an effort not to frown.

"Well, now that you two have met," Father Clark said, "I can leave you. I need to get over to the church and make some arrangements with the local parish priest. Mother Benedict is the expert on such moves as this, she has moved her school and teachers three times already."

Spur waved and the sallow faced priest lifted a shaking hand, then lowered it quickly and walked toward the front door. Spur did scowl at his back when the nun could not see him. If he didn't know better he would guess that Father Clark was in a hurry to get a long shot of whiskey to calm down his nerves.

Spur turned back to the Mother Superior who had not missed Spur's interest in the priest.

"Yes, we worry about him, too, Mr. McCoy. Father Clark is not a well man. We try to shield him as much as we can. That's partly why you and I will select what we need for this trip."

Mother Superior Mary Benedict was on the far side of forty, maybe five feet four inches tall and on the heavy side as if to assert her authority. She wore spectacles with wire rims for reading. When not wearing them, they hung on a thin chain around her neck.

"Should we sit down over there in the chairs, Mr. McCoy? I have a list we need to go over."

Spur went with her to the chairs, but before she could go on, he spoke first.

"Mother Superior, have you ever been this far west before?"

"No."

"Yet you want to move out in the wilds of New Mexico with six nuns and a sickly priest to start a new parish or a school?"

"Precisely, young man. The Lord has told us to go to the heathen. We must go and teach. We're a teaching order. We go where we are ordered to by the mother church. Our lives and our daily work as well as our immortal souls, are all in the care of the Lord."

"Mother Superior, have you ever killed a rattlesnake?"

She looked up sharply. "No, of course not. Snakes are God's creatures like all the rest of the animals."

"Out here, Mother Superior, it is far better to kill a rattlesnake than to let the snake kill you. Have you ever shot a firearm?"

"No, well, a long time ago I did." Her forehead creased, her eyes hooded. "Young man, are you deliberately trying to frighten me?"

"Frankly, yes. Between here and the Rio Grande lies some of the most desolate, barren, worthless, primitive, uninhabited, useless land in the entire nation. This is near the end of June. The temperature will be well over a hundred degrees most of the time during the day. That kind of heat hour after hour saps your strength, sucks the moisture out of your body, and can drive a man insane after only a few hours of exposure. This is a rugged trip for trail hardened cavalry soldiers with proven mounts. How are seven nuns going to withstand a long march like this?"

"Mr. McCoy. You have your orders. We have our orders. We do not question the instructions we get. Remember, the Lord is always there helping us. We have faith, and faith can move mountains."

"The mountains are no problem, Mother Superior. What worries me is if your faith will stop a razor sharp arrow fired by a Mescalero Apache who suddenly rises up out of the desert where he has covered himself with sand? Dozens of travelers and settlers get killed out here every year by the Mescaleros. They kill whites and enemy Indians for sport, they make war for amusement, they are vicious and treacherous by nature, by design and because of social customs."

Mother Superior Mary Benedict sat up straighter. "Faith is not supposed to stop arrows, Mr. McCoy. Faith gives us the will to find a *method* to stop the arrows, or better to prevent them ever being released. Faith and commitment and obedience give us the power to use our minds to solve our problems." She watched him for a moment.

"Now, no more questioning of our orders. We WILL be going across this land. We WILL do it successfully. Women and even nuns, or should I say *especially* nuns, are much stronger and resourceful than you may think. All six of the sisters are volunteers for this outpost. Two are former farm girls, two have actually shot firearms. We will overcome all obstacles, Mr. McCoy."

She waited, giving him a chance to reply. When he only grimly nodded at her she went on.

"Now, to the project. We have a rough map of the suggested route. This, of course, will be the primary responsibility of you and the guide we hire."

Spur looked at the four times folded piece of paper. The march led across the high plateau of Texas, into New Mexico, across the plains there and then slightly south to the city of Roswell, New Mexico. That was half way across. From there it turned north to a pass through the Rocky Mountains and on west to the Rio Grande river.

"Most of this territory is a virtual desert, Mother Superior. It gets from three to seven inches of rainfall in an entire year! Water holes normally there are dried up this time of the year."

"Enough, Mr. McCoy. We will need to know about this problem, so we can plan around it. All problems have solutions. Now, one more small item. Father Clark is not well. He is fragile and has other problems, but it is our duty to see him safely across this desert. I am in charge of the move. The money needed for the equipment is in my care and responsibility. This is at the direction of our bishop. Don't be too quick to judge Father Clark. He is a good man, and a fine priest. As you suggested, he tends to drink now and then, but for that problem too, we will find a solution.''

THREE

Spur McCoy stood, walked to the front window and looked into the street for a stormy pair of minutes. Seven woman and a whiskey priest and General Halleck wanted him to take them across the New Mexican deserts in the middle of the summer? It was suicide! It was ridiculous! They all were out of their minds. He would not go unless they had at least fifty troopers to guard the nuns against the Mescaleros. His mind was made up. He walked back to the upholstered couch where Mother Superior Benedict sat and dropped into the chair he had used before.

"This whole trip is absolutely unthinkable. The risks are too great. The weather will be horrendous, and I'll have seven women and a whiskey priest to take care of. The chances of making it through with only ten troopers as escort are not good. Maybe half of us would be alive when we reached the Rio Grande. Do you want to see three of your nuns dead before they get to the big river?"

"Naturally, Mr. McCoy, I do not wish that.

However, such an estimate is highly suspect since it is only your own. I work closely with a higher authority who has indicated this trip should be made. He will guide and care for and protect us. We will go across, with or without your help. I am perfectly capable of hiring a guard and a wagonmaster, contacting the army for the escort and moving out. So, right now is the time for you to decide. Either you defy your orders from Washington and walk away from here, or you accept the challenge of getting us through with as little trouble and as few injuries and casualties as possible."

Sister Mary Benedict looked sternly at the man before her. Spur could read nothing more in her eyes but determination. She would go by herself if she had to, with the nuns pulling the damn wagon!

"All right, I'll go only because I figure you will do it yourself if I don't. But I'm stipulating that we get twenty troopers as escort at Fort Houston outside of town."

Mother Benedict grinned. "Good, good. If you were French I would kiss you on both cheeks! As it is, a handshake should suffice." She held out her hand, which he saw was somewhat suntanned and he found out it was strong when she gripped his.

"Deal. Now you have some lists? Why don't we start with a wagon. I'd say a good strong Conestoga maybe two or three years old, with wooden bows and a heavy canvas top. We can go to the Wagon Works two blocks down. Should I get a buggy?"

"Goodness no. The good Lord gave me two

strong legs and feet to walk on. I have my funds, and I'm ready to go now." She stood up quickly and they went out to the steps, turned left and at once stepped over a cowboy sleeping peacefully on the boardwalk in front of the hotel. A puddle of vomit near his mouth had attracted a cloud of flies.

"Poor soul," Mother Superior said as she stepped over him. She looked at a pad of paper in her hand.

"You said a Conestoga, right? I'm hoping we can find one with a twelve or a fourteen foot box, one of the bigger freight wagon types if possible. That will give us more room for our supplies and the organ."

"An organ, Mother? We're taking an organ along?"

"Yes, a pedal pump kind. They are relatively new, but we had one donated. Then there is the bell for the new church. It is the heaviest thing we have. So we need a wagon with a carrying capacity of about six thousand to sixty-five hundred pounds."

"And eight oxen to pull it," Spur said. "I'm afraid we won't find a freight wagon that size. A ten or twelve footer will be more likely."

They stepped down off the boardwalk into the dust of the street. Mother Superior lifted her habit as she stepped over fresh horse droppings. A thousand flies scattered as they walked past. She ignored them all, a set, determined smile on her face.

Stepping up to the boardwalk on the far side of the street, the long black skirt snagged on a splintered pine plank and stopped her.

Spur knelt and unhooked the heavy cloth.

"One more thing, Mother Superior. You and your nuns must wear more practical clothes. I would suggest pants and shirts for all of you. These heavy habits will be deathly hot, and they are too bulky and cumbersome for the travel and camp work we'll be doing."

"Impossible. The order dictates quite plainly our habit. We would need a release from the head of the order in Chicago before we could alter our dress."

Spur stopped and scowled. "Sister, I thought you were the smart one here, the practical, efficient person who could manage people and situations and get good things accomplished. You just failed your first test. Have you ever climbed up on a Conestoga front driver's seat in your habit? Ever sat a horse with those bulky multiple skirts on? Have you worn your head and neck covering during hundred and ten degree weather for twenty or thirty days outside?

"To make this trip safely we first must be extremely lucky, then we must be damned smart and take advantage of every possible chance we have, and third, we must be as basic and practical as possible. What does your logical, practical, efficient mind tell you how your people should dress for the trip?"

Mother Superior Benedict smiled, took off her steel rimmed glasses and cleaned them with a soft white handkerchief. When she put the spectacles back on, she nodded.

"Of course, Mr. McCoy, you are right. We will

buy trousers and shirts and alter them to fit before we leave."

"Thank you, Mother Superior."

"I'm not always stubborn, am I? You were right to appeal to my practical nature. That will usually win a tough argument with me—at least for this trip where you are the expert."

They found the Lubbock Wagon Works a half block later. It was a well established firm, and made wagons, mostly for the farmers and ranchers. The owner had a dozen used wagons, but only one Conestoga. It had wooden bows and a heavy canvas top.

Spur examined it, checked the date burned into the front of the box. It had been made six years ago.

Amos, the owner of the firm, saw Spur checking the big wagon and he walked over.

"That Connie is sound as a dollar, Mr. McCoy. Army drove her in here two years ago then she was too big for their regular rigs so they traded me."

Spur checked the box, twelve foot. She had two and a half inch wide steel rimmed wheels, standard three foot eight inchers in front but on back larger four foot ten inch wheels with nearly a three inch steel rim around the wooden spokes and outer wooden circle. He liked the rig at once.

"How much?" Spur asked. "Remember, this is for the church. Should be a good discount."

"In Boston, that Connie would cost you a hundred and twenty dollars new. But out here, and since it's the church and all, I could let her go for say, ninety-five."

"Beat up and six years old," Spur said. "Needs two new spokes in that front wheel, and we'll need a stiff tongue and a gear brake. Might go as high as sixty dollars."

"Hell, man, I paid eighty-five!" Amos stirred a circle in the dust with his toe. "Well, seeing it's the church and all, I'll fix up those things on her and let you steal it from me for seventy-five."

Mother Superior Benedict walked up while they were talking. "Amos, I am surprised at you, trying to make so much profit on a sale to the church. Come down to seventy dollars, fix everything Mr. Spur suggests, throw in two lead ropes twenty feet long and you have a sale."

Amos laughed and agreed.

Spur examined the wagon critically, found one more spoke that was about to break and saw that they fixed everything, then installed the gear brake and made sure that it worked. The stiff tongue would be easier to hitch up. Mother Superior gave Amos forty dollars and would pay the rest on delivery in two hours.

As they left, Amos was smiling, yelling at two of his men to get to work on the old Connie.

Spur and the nun went to the Bedlow Livery Stable next. He picked out two teams of mules that were used to working together, haggled the price down to fifteen dollars each, then bought one more at the same price. While he was there he picked out a saddle horse for himself, bought a saddle and a rope, a boot for a Spencer and talked the livery man into throwing in a pair of saddle bags.

Most liveries in that part of the country had a

tack shop at one side. This one did too, so Spur and Mother Superior arranged for complete harness and reins for the two teams. Spur harnessed two of the mules and led them to the wagon works. When the Conestoga was ready, Spur hitched up the team and met Mother Superior at the general store. The mules pulled well and the Conestoga handled like she was new.

It took them nearly three hours to select, buy and load the supplies for the trip. Spur and the merchant worked out the shopping list.

For 310 miles they figured 15 miles a day or from 20 to 25 days. They took food and supplies for 30 days just to be safe. They stocked up on bacon, beans, flour, sugar, coffee, rice, rolled oats, dried apples, raisins and dried apricots, three sacks of potatoes, a 50 gallon drum for drinking water and Spur added three Spencer 7-shot rifles and 500 cartridges.

"Absolutely no firearms!" Mother Superior said.

The merchant guffawed and then apologized. "Sister, you just ain't never been on the desert, and you don't know the Mescaleros. With them you shoot first if you see them, but mostly you'll never see them, and when you do, half the time you're dead anyway so it don't matter. You going out there to Roswell without rifles is like lining up them six nuns of yours and shooting them out there in the public square. Only thing is, it would be more merciful for you to shoot them here and now than to let the Mescal's have them. Begging your pardon, Sister, but you have no idea what they do to white women before they kill them."

Mother Superior Benedict stared at the merchant and slowly nodded. "I'm afraid you're right. Yes, let's put in six of the rifles, and a thousand rounds."

Spur McCoy turned so she couldn't see him and grinned.

When they got the food, camping and cooking supplies on board, they drove to the Western Freighters and Spur looked at the organ, the three-foot wide bell, and the stack of boxes that had to go on the wagon.

The freighters helped them load, putting the heavy bell and organ in the middle of the wagon, then packing the boxes and other gear around them. Spur opened boxes and consulted with Mother Superior. They found eight cartons of tracts and literature that they decided the would donate to the local parish. They were still overloaded.

Spur went through the boxes again, found three more the nun said they could leave, then he unloaded the tent and took it back to the store. They just had no room for it.

Spur and Mother Superior picked out two pair of pants and two shirts for each of the nuns. They had approximate sizes, but all would need to be altered to be practical. Sister Ruth could do that, she was a whiz with a needle and thread, Mother Superior said.

It was nearing four o'clock when Spur realized they had not eaten at noon. He checked the wagon again, making sure the food was placed where it would be available, that the camping and cooking gear were on the outside. The water barrel was in back, well wedged into place.

He sent Sister Mary Benedict back to the hotel to rest while he drove to the Wagon Works and bought a spare front wheel, which they wired in place under the center of the wagon box. Front wheels broke more often than rears, and it would be practical to have a spare. Spur admitted he was not the best wheel wright in the world, so he didn't want to be repairing a wheel on the trail.

Spur parked the Conestoga at the side of the hotel and put the mules in the small stable at the rear. Once more he walked to the livery and picked out three saddle horses for the nuns to ride. He found the most gentle animals he could that looked like they could stand the long trail. That meant three more bridles and saddles.

After he settled up the bill for the mounts and gear, he rode his own bay gelding back to the hotel and tied him up outside. Spur had agreed to meet Mother Superior in her hotel lobby and they would go to the small restaurant across the street for supper. She said it would cost half as much as eating at the hotel.

He went to his own hotel room, washed up, combed his hair, then checked his six-gun. It was clean and oiled and ready for the range again.

Spur put on his low crowned brown hat with the string of Mexican silver pieces around it, and headed for the other big hotel. He was not overly anxious to see the rest of his charges for this trip, but there was no way to put it off now.

He found the nuns, all in their habits, clustered around the shorter and stockier

Mother Superior. Father Clark was not with them.

Spur came up at the side of the flock and cleared his throat. One of the nuns looked up and smiled. She had deep brown eyes and a softly white face.

"Mother . . ." she said.

Mother Benedict turned and saw Spur and smiled.

"Sisters, look around here and be thankful. This is the gentleman who is going to help us get across this unfriendly land to the Rio Grande."

Spur watched them turn and look at him. He saw six round faces bound tightly by the cowl like head covering, making them look like peas in a pod.

"Mr. McCoy, I'll introduce you to each Sister. We won't expect you to remember names just yet. Over here we have Sister Mary Cecilia, then Sister Mary Francis, Sister Mary Joseph, Sister Mary Ruth, Sister Mary Maria and Sister Mary Teresa."

The last nun turned when her name was called and stared at him. A tentative smile edged around her mouth, and Spur thought he was going to drop straight through a crack in the floor. The same darting soft blue eyes, the crinkling nose and the sensuous mouth. She was the Teresa he had tumbled with in bed last night! He had made love with a nun!

Her eyes were laughing at him, enjoying his surprise and his discomfort.

Each of the nuns had nodded and said a few words to him, and now it was Sister Teresa's turn.

"Mr. McCoy. I'm sure you are the man to get us across the desert. It will be a hard job, but I know you'll be able to do it."

To the rest of them it was idle chatter, but to Spur the loaded words hit him like two kicks to the crotch.

Somehow he collected himself enough to thank them all and suggest they go have supper. They went across the street and down a block to a small family restaurant. Mother Superior had arranged it. They sat together at a long table in the back of the room and all had the same food, vegetable soup, crackers and cheese sandwiches. They drank milk.

The meal was over quickly and Spur found himself next to Sister Teresa as they walked back to the hotel.

"Lovely last night," she whispered back as he stepped to the side to let the others go up the hotel steps.

"That's a challenge!" she said softly as he held the door for her as the last nun walked inside.

Spur spoke to Mother Superior for a moment in the lobby.

"Tonight I'm looking for the best guide I can find. Nobody is going to be wild to take this kind of job. What do you have in your budget for wages?"

"What is a fair price?" she asked.

"Fifty dollars."

"No more. Our funds are limited." She sighed. "I'm sorry, Mr. McCoy, I did not mean to be sharp with you, but I am starting to be concerned about money."

"I'll do the best I can."

He went first to the sheriff, but the lawman had no ideas about scouts or guides across to the Rio Grande.

"Been talk about the Mescaleros getting nasty again," the sheriff said. His name was Prescott, and he looked like he could handle the big Colt on his thigh.

"The Mescaleros are always nasty when they aren't being vicious or treacherous," Spur said. He left his name and hotel room number in case the sheriff heard of anyone looking.

He tried the bars. The first two proved to provide fairly cold beer but no scouts.

In the third one a young halfbreed said he knew the land, but if the Mescaleros ever captured him, they would use him as a human sacrifice to their gods. He was staying as far away from Mescalero territory as possible.

The fourth bar and gambling hall he found a grizzled man in his forties who said he would make the trip to Roswell but no farther.

"Cost you two hundred to get to Roswell," the man said. He was half drunk, but his eyes shone with a horse trader's gleam.

"Can't even offer you a hundred," Spur said.

"You do and you got a guide," the man said. "Billbrough is the name. You want me, just put in a word with the bar man here. He can find me. I've lived all through that area, but the damn Mescals are going in for more raiding than they have in years. A caution, my new friend. Whether you hire me or not be sure that you watch your ass out there."

FOUR

Spur McCoy checked in the last drinking parlor in the town of Lubbock slightly before midnight. This one had boards laid across saw-horses for the bar, sawdust on the floor and no ice for the beer.

Two men at the bar said they would be glad to scout the trail and lead the wagon over to the Rio Grande. Both were over sixty-five, toothless, wasted by long years in the outdoors, and Spur was sure that neither one could sit a horse.

He found no other candidates for the job, left his half a warm beer on the board top, and talked with the apron.

The man was thin and wheezing. His nose ran and his thinning hair showed brown splotches on his head. He wiped his nose on his sleeve and shook his head.

"No chance to get a scout for that trip now. Too damn many Mescals out there lifting scalps. Last week we lost two wagons trying to run across."

Spur thanked him and headed outside. He kicked at the boardwalk as he moved back to his hotel. Tomorrow he would make the circuit again, and talk to the store owners. The livery stable man might have an idea. Yeah, tomorrow.

McCoy was tired when he unlocked his hotel room door and pushed it open. He scratched a match and lit the lamp, then shoved the door closed with his foot.

Just after the door latched he heard a deadly click as a six-gun hammer cocked ready for fire. His back was to the sound, both hands still near the lamp.

"Can I turn around, or are you going to shoot me in the back?" the Secret Service man asked his unseen opponent.

"Turn around slowly, hands way up," the voice said. It was a woman.

He turned gradually, making sure she would not shoot. His head moved faster and he saw her sitting in a chair next to the window, the ugly black muzzle of a .44 angled over the back of the chair and centered on his chest.

She was dark, with long black hair, but her face looked part Indian to go with her more obvious Mexican heritage. A Breed. He had never seen her before.

Spur stopped turning and smiled. "So, you're not here to rob me, or kill me. What do you want?"

"Just to see the surprised look on your face when that hammer clicked back," she said quickly, then laughed. She let the hammer down softly on the weapon and it vanished. "You can put your hands down now. You're tall."

42

"Yes, and you're short. My name is Spur McCoy, but you must know that. Who are you?"

"You ask a lot of damn questions, don't you?"

"Bad habit of mine."

She left the chair and he saw she wore man's pants that fit tightly across her sleek young body. She was barely five feet tall, slender but with a white blouse that punched outward. The Breed had black bangs hanging across her forehead. Now she sat on the edge of the bed closer to the lamp. Her brown eyes were wide set, cheekbones high leaving little hollows in her cheeks. Her mouth was small and cupid curved. It was a pretty face. He guessed she was eighteen, maybe nineteen.

He saw the .44 in her right sided holster.

"You always pack so much firepower?"

"When I'm in town. Most folks here don't like me."

"Just because you have a mixed racial heritage?"

"You noticed."

"I always notice pretty girls who sneak into my room at midnight and hold a gun on me."

She laughed. "I think I'm going to like you, Spur McCoy. My name is Chiquita. You are looking for a guide to take your Catholic missionaries over to the Rio Grande."

"That's true, and so far I've been looking without much success."

"I'll do it. I know the country better than anyone in the area except the Mescaleros. I am half Mescalero and spent ten years out there. I know the water holes, the trails, the traps and the blind canyons. There is no one in town who

43

can get you through Mescalero country as safely as I can."

"Besides all that, you're modest," he said smiling.

"No, I'm good. I also think like a Mescalero does, so I can avoid them, go where they are not."

"Are they raiding again?"

"More than ever. They stopped two wagons a week ago. Nobody came back. The burned out hulks are still out there. I could have led those people safely across."

Spur frowned as he watched her. She was small, but a white hot determination burned from her dark eyes. Also she was half Mescal. That could be tremendously important.

"If you lead the roundeyes, you are not on good terms with your people."

"No, for several reasons. They do not consider me a part of their tribe. I am *Woman in Two Camps,* and accepted in neither. So I live as I can."

"How much for the trip?"

"I should charge you two hundred, but I know that drunk roundeye said he would go for a hundred to Roswell. That's only half way. I will go to Roswell for eighty dollars in gold. I do not trust the Yankee paper money."

"That's three months wages for a cowhand. Clerk in a store works two months for that much gold."

"But neither of them has to dodge the Apache arrows or bullets. Many Mescaleros have rifles now and they have learned to shoot well. They raid wagons for more rifles and for bullets. I know where they hide, where they wait, where they hunt and how they move. I am your life-savor for the nuns. You know what Mescalero raiders do to white women. Think what would happen to the Catholic nuns."

"I know, I've been there." He watched her. She showed him a stern Indian stare, her bargaining look.

"I'll recommend you to the boss tomorrow. Can you be at the Texas Ranch House Hotel tomorrow at ten o'clock? I'll introduce you to Mother Superior Benedict."

Chiquita smiled. "A nun giving you orders. You must like that."

"Depends on the orders."

She moved toward the door and suddenly a four-inch knife materialized in her right hand and she tapped it on his chest.

"Don't get any funny ideas, gringo. If you touch my body, I will cut your heart out." She slipped past him and opened the door. "Of course another time, another place, who knows? Tomorrow at ten, I'll be there." She stepped out the door and closed it behind her.

McCoy watched the space for a moment. The door did not reopen. He went over and locked it, then sat down on the bed. It had been a long, tough day. A whiskey priest, a nun who scoffed at her vow of chastity, and now a pretty little Breed with a Mescalero mind and a Mexican hot temper who was going to be his guide and scout.

It was turning out to be one hell of an unlikely group of people to make a dangerous trip through the Apache Mescaleros who were riled up and raiding everything that moved through their traditional territory.

Maybe he could get thirty army troopers for escort duty, this being a church group and with seven women. Maybe.

Spur got undressed and into bed. Tonight was for catching up on his sleep. He didn't get much last night.

The next morning Spur slept in until almost eight o'clock, an unheard of time for him. He ate a leisurely breakfast downstairs, then made sure the two mules in the small stable behind the hotel had hay and a bite of oats. He sat on the steps outside the Ranch House Hotel in his blue jeans, blue striped shirt and a black leather vest. He tipped the brown, low crowned hat back on his head and soaked up some early morning sun. It would be a blistering ninety degrees today in the shade. He had been in that kind of heat before.

He could ride out to Camp Houston and check on the military, but an early visit would make no difference. When they came to pick up the escort it would be ready or not or doubled or halved according to the unpredictable orders of the Division of Texas Army Headquarters. He pulled his hat down over his eyes and relaxed.

Ten minutes before the set meeting time, someone flipped his hat off his head. He came up, his hand hovering over his six-gun tied down on his right hip.

"Take it careful, hombre," a small voice said. "You are as safe as if you were in your own bed."

Chiquita sat down beside him. She had on the

same dark brown pants but now a brown blouse that was not quite as tight as the white one. It still revealed where Chiquita had put in a lot of her growth, rather than height.

"Are you through staring so we can meet the nuns?" Chiquita said, her voice layered with impatience.

"Might just as well, it's time." Spur stood, stretched, waved toward the door and walked behind the small woman. He noticed that a low crowned black, wide brimmed hat hung down her back on a black cord. She wore boots, not moccasins.

When Spur pushed open the door to the hotel, the desk clerk looked up, his face darkened and he started toward Chiquita.

Spur McCoy lifted one hand and pointed his finger at the man, who glanced nervously at him as Spur touched Chiquita's shoulder and moved her to the front window where Mother Superior Benedict stood. The clerk scowled and retreated, throwing angry looks at Spur.

The Mother Superior saw them coming, she turned and smiled, and Spur felt something pass between the two women before either spoke.

"Mother Superior, this is Chiquita," Spur said when they stopped in front of her.

The nun spoke quickly in fluent Spanish that Spur had trouble following. It was a pleased, cordial greeting, and she reached out one hand and clasped the smaller browner one.

Chiquita replied in Spanish.

Then the Breed switched to English.

"Mother, I would like to be your scout through the Mescalero country. I am half

47

Mescal myself and know their ways. Mr. McCoy has approved and my price is $70. I hope that is not too much."

There was no bargaining, Mother Superior Benedict nodded quickly. "Yes, that is agreeable. Can you start first thing in the morning?"

"Of course."

"Next order of business is to have Chiquita look over our rig and our gear," Spur said. He looked at her. "You might have some suggestions."

"Yes, good. Let's go now."

"You can meet the sisters later," Mother Benedict said.

"Five-thirty start in the morning?" Chiquita asked.

The other two agreed and Spur and Chiquita left for the small stable behind the hotel. The night stable man had watched the wagon for them, and nothing was missing.

Chiquita spent an hour going over each item in the loaded rig and when she was done she called to McCoy.

"We need another twenty gallon keg of water, and a two gallon cask of whiskey. If we get in trouble we throw out the cask of whiskey and within two hours every Mescalero brave on the raid will be falling down drunk!"

Spur laughed.

"It has worked before. Whiskey is like a poison to the Mescaleros. Oh, we should take some dried beef, twenty pounds. It will last for months."

Spur agreed and they went to the store for the supplies, brought them back and loaded them on board. They hid the whiskey so Mother Superior would not see it, and especially so that Father Clark could not find it.

When they were done they sat on a stack of blankets near the back of the covered wagon.

"Any good job interview should include some background," Spur said.

"Finally you ask." She stared at him with a frank, open expression. "I will tell you, I am not ashamed of my parents. My mother was captured by the Mescaleros on a raid of a small Mexican village across the border. She was so pretty the capturing brave kept her as his second wife.

"A second wife is important to most Mescalero braves. The women do all the work, and a second wife can make things easier for the first wife. Also my father had only two daughters, and he wanted a son. My younger brother fulfilled his dreams and he let us go back to the Mexican village. But he kept his son and raised him as a Mescalero."

"But the Mexican villagers drove you and your mother out, right?"

She looked at him quickly. "You know a lot about my country, my people. Yes, they said my mother was not fit to live among them. They hate the Mescals. Since I was a Breed, they despised me ten times as much as they did her. I have known much hatred and now I am a squaw in three camps, and can live in peace in none of them."

"Times change, people change."

"But I will not live long enough for that. The hatred killed my mother when I was still ten.

Two gringo nuns found me in a street begging and took me in. They raised me. It was a small village in Texas near the border, away from the Mescaleros country. I have known many wonderful nuns . . . and a few whiskey priests."

"We have one on this trip."

"I heard." She lifted her black brows. "I also hear that he spends his days in the chapel praying, and his nights slapping around the whores in a bordello."

FIVE

Father Wilbur Clark sat up in the strange bed and glanced around the unfamiliar room. Jesus! This place looked like a whorehouse! He had been amusing himself lately by swearing in his thoughts. It had produced hours of euphoric pleasures for him.

He inventoried the bedroom with his eyes. It was fancy, with a real brass bed frame and elaborate head and feet. The walls were papered in a bright flower pattern, with border strip four inches wide circling the room a foot below the ceiling which was papered with a softer, more relaxed print.

The one window was draped luxuriously with two lined curtains that hung to the floor and were swagged back on each side with luxuriant pink ropes that ended in showy tassles. A soft white thin material covered the window which was hidden by a pull down blind.

The cream colored blind had been painted with a scene of a pleasant mountain meadow. Definitely a woman's room.

It still looked like a whorehouse. The closet was jammed with fancy clothes and on a dressing table he saw all sorts of creams and lotions and colors for applying rouge and makeup to the face.

It not only looked like a room in a whorehouse, it was, and not just a crib, the room that belonged to the madam herself.

Someone snored softly beside him.

Father Clark looked down at the henna red haired woman. Her face was flat and plain, her nose too large and lips too tight. Now her mouth hung open inducing the snore. He reached over and pushed up her chin holding her mouth closed. The snoring stopped. He figured she was about forty years old.

She lay on top of the sheet as naked as he was. Her small breasts were now flattened against her chest. In her sleep she curled one hand between her legs and moaned softly in pleasure.

He looked to the other side and saw the younger woman awake beside him. She was softly blonde, even to the blonde thatch over her golden triangle. Her breasts were two hand size, and still looked large enough when she lay on her back. She was no more than twenty. She said her name was Lily.

She winked at him. "Ready to spend another five dollars?" she said, her pretty face grinning, strange blue eyes quick and ready.

"What about my discount?"

"You used that up last night," she said, her voice only a whisper. "Better idea. Bet you five you can't stick yours in old Gert there without waking her up."

Wilbur Clark laughed softly. "That's like taking candy from a whore, a Lily whore. Watch me."

He softly touched Gert's breasts, then petted them, using a little more pressure all the time until he was kneading them firmly bringing small gasps of pleasure from the sleeping woman.

Then he moved one hand to her legs and massaged her inner thighs until she moaned softly and moved her hand, then edged her legs apart slowly. His hand rubbed the black fur over her prize until she moaned again, then his fingers found her slot and teased it a moment, then toyed with the already wet and juicy labia.

Clark noticed that Lily moved closer to him, now she had her hands at his crotch working her delicate magic on his shaft which was almost erect. She bent and licked his throbbing tool and grinned.

"I think you're ready," she said.

Gert moved her hips slowly around and around now as his fingers kept up a steady stroking of her labia and a casual touch of her clitoris.

Clark eased Gert's legs apart more, lifted her knees and settled between them, then slowly he touched her red, swollen lips with his shaft and slid it forward.

Gert sighed and thrust her hips upward, then she yelped softly as he lanced past the first tight muscle and slid gently into her until their pelvic bones touched.

He grinned at Lily.

"You owe me five dollars, younger whore,"

Clark said.

Lily shook her head. "Gert has been awake since the first time you touched her tits. It's a game we play with old bastards like you."

"Lily, I'm not going to pay you a dime," Clark said. He watched Gert and she didn't move. "That proves she's sleeping!" he whispered. "You owe me five bucks, right now!"

Lily rolled off the bed. "Finish what you got started, old man, then we'll talk."

Clark looked back at the woman under him and snorted, then he pumped hard a dozen times, exploded inside her and came away. Gert still lay where she had been.

"I was awake all the time, Padre," Gert said, bursting out with a raucous laugh. She sat up. "You two were whispering so loud it would wake up anybody. I knew the first time you touched my tits, so you owe her the five dollars."

Father Clark slapped Gert on one washed out, painted cheek, knocking her backwards on the bed.

"Bitch! Damned whore! I didn't come in here to get swindled by a pair of trollops! I paid enough last night to last me the rest of the day. That was the deal. Thirty dollars for the two of you for twenty-four hours."

"The deal is off when you get rough," Gert said. "If I call Amos he'll throw you butt bare right out the second story window, collar or no."

Clark slapped her again and she tried to roll away from him. He dove on top of her pinning her to the bed. Lily jumped on his back, her fingernails making long scratches down his shoulders and back. Then she beat on him with her small fists.

"Get away from her! Let Gert go!" She turned and found a heavy porcelain pitcher on the dressing table and swung it at Clark. He dodged and the pitcher hit Gert on the side of the head. She slammed backwards on the bed, unconscious.

"You killed her!" Clark roared. "You slut! You murderer! You killed poor Gert!"

Lily dropped the pitcher, staring at the still form on the bed, then she fell beside her on her stomach, weeping hysterically.

Clark watched her a minute, then moved behind her, lifted her hips off the bed and began stroking her soft buttocks.

"No!" Lily said. "No!"

Clark spanked her six times as she squealed.

"Lily, old Gert isn't dead, you just knocked her out. Remember you're both bought and paid for until noon today. You got to do damn well what I tell you, woman."

"Then Gert is not dead, not hurt bad?"

"Hell no, you just grazed her with the pitcher. Now get on your hands and knees and hang them beauties into my face. Like to get half smothered with them, unless I eat my way free."

"She's going to be all right?" Lily demanded.

"Yeah, yeah. Just knocked her senseless. She'll be coming around as horny as ever in a few minutes. Now hang them tits of yours for me to chew on!"

She went down on all fours and he crawled under her, licking and chewing.

Lily shrugged. "You're ready to pop again.

How long had it been since you'd done a woman?"

"Fucking near a year. Kept me in a cell, a monastic cell, only they had the key. All because I drank a little and they caught me fucking this fourteen year old one day when she came in with some questions. I answered her big question!"

He pushed Lily away and knelt behind her.

"Oh, no, please, not there!"

"Why not, you been had there before."

"It hurts. Really, I'm not made quite the way most women are, and it really hurts."

"That's too bad, I want your asshole, now."

He tried to mount her and she yelled and crawled across the bed. Clark went after her. As he did, Gert lifted up with the heavy porcelain pitcher and swung it at Clark. She missed his head and slammed it into his shoulder.

He growled and sat up on the bed, holding his shoulder. Then he slid off the bed and found his pants. He took out a knife and opened a four-inch blade.

"Time we start playing the game for keeps!"

Lily saw the knife and ran for the door. He jumped in front of her and swung the knife toward her breasts. She sagged backward and fell on the bed.

Gert slid off the bed and as Clark advanced on Lily, Gert opened the door and screamed for Amos, then ran naked down the hall screaming his name.

Clark let her go. He hovered over the naked girl on the bed.

"You have not been nice to me, Lily. I bought and paid for you and you were not nice. So I'll have to give you a lesson—one slashed breast.''

The knife darted out, sliced a two inch gash in her right breast. Blood sprung up and flowed a red river.

Lily screamed, then put her hand over her breast to slow the bleeding. She scurried off the far side of the bed, but then was in the corner of the room.

"Lily, you have been a bad girl. You have sinned in the sight of man and God, and you must be punished. I am the right hand of the Lord. I am his mighty sword that strikes down all evil doers. I am a warrior of the Lord!"

He sprang forward, the knife arcing through the air toward Lily's throat. She fell backwards screaming.

Clark stopped and stared at her naked body on the floor. She was so lovely, such a marvelous sex machine! But she could not be spared. She had to die. He was the warrior of the Lord! It would be like last time. She would pay for her sins, and his own debt would be paid as well.

He moved forward.

Lily crowded backward, sitting on the floor, edging toward the wall. Looking for something to protect herself with. There was nothing, not even a pillow. The chair! She pushed it at him and he swept it aside.

"Lily, you have sinned," he said solemnly. "You have sinned before the most holy God!" He knelt in front of her. Lily pressed against the wall. Clark held the knife out so she could see streaks of her own blood on it.

Blood ran down her breast to her stomach.

"Lily, you must die for your sins!"

He lifted the knife and began to swing it toward her.

"May God have mercy on your soul!"

A big black fist slammed into the side of Father Clark's head before the knife reached Lily. Amos's blow pounded Clark to the side and against the bed. His head hit the oak sideboard and he slumped unconscious to the floor.

Lily trembled in shock. She blubbered in anguished hysteria, and Gert rushed in with water and a towel, bandages and a bottle of whiskey.

"Drink," she said. Lily took a shot of the booze, then Gert wiped the blood away from her breast. She sloshed the whiskey over her slash and Lily passed out from the pain.

Amos gathered up Father Clark's clothes, hoisted him over his shoulder and carried the priest down the back stairs. He knew what to do. He walked down two blocks then to the alley door of the county jail. He knocked twice on the door and a few moments later had deposited Father Clark with his clothes in a back cell.

The deputy sheriff listened to the story and shook his head. Someone would be coming to get him out. But first the priest had to sober up and pay for the damages to both property and to the dance hall girl, Lily, who was extremely popular in town, especially with the sheriff.

SIX

Spur McCoy edged his mount up to the side of the Conestoga and looked over at Mother Superior Benedict. Her habit was gone. She wore overalls and a too large shirt over them. Now Spur could see that her hair was a gentle brown, cut short and combed back. There was a distinct white band around her forehead below her hairline where the habit had covered her.

Mother Benedict took a pocket watch from her overalls and looked at it, then glanced up at Spur.

"He's not coming, is he?" Spur asked. The nun shook her head and frowned.

"As you can imagine, this has happened before. I'm afraid you'll have to go find him."

"May not be hard. Heard there was a fight earlier this morning in a . . . saloon. Wait for me."

Spur kicked his horse and it moved down the street toward the sheriff's office. That was always the best place to start. He had enjoyed watching the sun come up that morning as they

59

put the final touches on the Conestoga and the nuns got used to their overalls and blue jeans. The shirts were much too large for most of them, and a little small for others, still they served their purpose.

Chiquita had been everywhere, checking the shoes on the mules and the horses. That was one reason they were held up. She sent one riding horse back for a new shoe to replace the one that was about to come off.

They had been ready to roll an hour late at 6:30 A.M., only the priest was not to be found.

Mother Benedict had left a note on his door the night before telling him to be packed and in the lobby at five that morning. She said the note was still on his door this morning and he was not in his room.

Chiquita told Spur the priest had been at the Two Dollar saloon the night before with two whores. He might still be there.

When Spur stopped in front of the Lubbock County Sheriff's Office, he was just in time to meet the sheriff coming to work. Inside the sheriff nodded to Spur.

"What can I do for you?" the lawman asked.

"Missing a spare priest. Could he be a guest of the county?"

The all night deputy came in from the cells.

"He sure as hell is, Sheriff. Came in about two hours ago drunk as a skunk and passed out. Amos brought him naked as a jay bird. I think he finally got himself dressed."

"What kind of charges?" Spur asked.

"He cut up Miss Lily over at the Two Dollar. Lot of folks around town gonna be unhappy

60

about that. Cut one . . . breast."

"It bad, Ira?"

"Don't reckon. Doc said he pulled the cut together and tied it up. Probably be only a thin scar. About two inches long he said."

The sheriff turned to Spur.

"You gonna pay the fine?"

"I guess I'll have to."

"Going rate is ten dollars an inch, plus ten dollars court costs. Thirty dollars."

"Any discount for the clergy?" Spur asked. All three men laughed and Spur gave the sheriff a twenty and a ten dollar bill.

"Roll him out," the sheriff said. "This whiskey priest of yours is a sick man. Better take care of him. If you don't one of these days he's gonna kill a girl, and then he'll hang for sure. His collar won't stop that trap from springing or that hangman's knot from breaking his neck."

"Sheriff, I think you're right," Spur said.

Five minutes later Father Wilbur Clark came through the door squinting. He was both hung over and wrung out. His collar was not straight and his black attire rumpled and dirty.

Outside, Spur pointed the direction, and walked beside him a ways.

"Clark, let's you and me get something all talked out. I tried to get Mother Superior Benedict to leave you here to rot, but she insisted you come. A promise she made your bishop. Frankly, I don't think you'll make it across the country we have to travel. One thing I want you to understand. To me you're no priest, I'll call you by your last name only. On this trip I'm the boss, you do exactly what I tell you to do because there will probably be somebody's life hanging in the balance. Now, do we understand each other?"

For a moment Father Clark frowned at Spur.

"Sir, I answer only to my bishop, not to you. I'll act as I please, do as I please. I am in command of this group, if you don't like that, then I sug . . ."

Spur slammed a right cross into the priestly jaw. The blow knocked him into the dust.

The priest sat up, felt his jaw, and spat at Spur.

"Now, Clark, do we understand each other?"

"Absolutely," Father Clark said. "And you may expect that the first chance I have I will discredit you and send you packing. If that doesn't work, I'll tie you up and castrate you. Enjoy the trip, McCoy, but you better always be watching over your shoulder and sleeping light."

Spur was tempted to use the rope on his saddle and drag the priest back to the Conestoga, but he decided it would make it more difficult to deal with the ladies on the wagon. He rode behind the man as they walked the five hundred yards to the covered wagon.

Chiquita had three of the nuns on horseback. Two were farm girls who had ridden before. The nuns were to ride on each side of the wagon and look out for holes and problems. Chiquita saw Spur load the priest on the wagon, then she took off west out of town, heading for Roswell, New Mexico.

Mother Superior Benedict had driven teams

before. She had a little trouble with the double team, but soon learned how to hold the reins. The mules were steady, and slightly faster than oxen would have been. Both teams had worked together before and soon they settled into a steady pace that carried the big wagon across the three thousand foot high plateau of western Texas.

Spur had not spoken with Sister Mary Teresa that morning. Both had projects to finish. Now he was glad she was inside the wagon. The army post, Camp Houston, was four miles west of town. They should reach it in an hour. Getting the mules settled down and into the routine would mean slow progress the first day or two.

As the big Conestoga rolled along, he checked the rig. The wheels were sounding right and Mother Benedict understood how to work the brake.

He spotted a small tear in the canvas top that he would have sewn up as soon as they stopped. Sisters Francis, Joseph and Maria were enjoying their horseback riding. That too would get old quickly.

Spur trotted up to where Chiquita sat on her horse watching the country. She heard him coming but did not turn.

"Any problems?" he asked.

She shook her head. "Not this close to town and the Army. I can see their smoke ahead, just over that slight rise."

"Yes, good idea," Spur said. "I'll ride forward and check out our escort, and try to get it doubled. Would you object to that?"

"Tripled might be better. If we get hit by

Mescalero, it means I have not done my job. I don't want to fight our way through. It's much safer to slip past the Indians than it is to fight them."

"I agree, but troops are specified on my orders." He touched his hat brim in a salute. "I'll try to meet you with the escort before you reach the fort."

Spur touched the bay with his toes and she moved ahead sharply. The army. It had been a lot of years since he had seen a full time soldier. He carried a card detailing his current rank as that of Lt. Colonel, unassigned and on temporary duty. He would use the card if he needed it.

The army being what it was, he probably would have to use it. He rode the remaining three miles to the camp quickly, and came past a small stream with trees nearby. It would be a good place to camp if it were not so early in the morning. morning.

The army camp was not a fort. There were a scattering of fifteen or twenty buildings, all made of native stone and mortar with flat roofs, a minimum of windows and those with heavy shutters that could be closed and locked in place from the inside.

There were six long buildings for the enlisted men's barracks, five officers' houses, and a large mess hall and kitchen that probably also served as a meeting center. Spur saw the guidon of the 3rd Calvary fluttering by the gate, a formal affair that had no fence nor fort on either side of it.

What was the 3rd doing up here? Last he remembered they were stationed several hundred miles south at Fort Davis. He shrugged and rode up to the sentry.

"Colonel McCoy to see your commander, Corporal."

The corporal saluted and called for the sergeant of the guard.

A moment later a proper greeting occurred as the sergeant rode out, saluted formally and led Spur to the commandant's quarters. It was the largest of the stone buildings. There wasn't a bush, flower or tree anywhere in the camp. The sergeant knocked on the door, opened it and stepped inside.

McCoy followed. The building was a residence with an *office* room up front. A large American flag with thirty-eight stars in the corner covered half the rear wall. The inside of the room had been plastered and painted. It was army through and through. A brass spittoon sat to the side ready for use by both the men in front and behind a large desk.

The officer behind the desk rose and smiled. He was short, stocky, and held major's oak leaves on his shoulders. His uniform was clean, pressed and precise. A thin moustache adorned his upper lip and he stared over half glasses.

"Sir, may I present Colonel McCoy," the sergeant said. "Colonel McCoy, this is Major Donaldson, Camp Houston commander."

Major Donaldson saluted. Spur returned the salute, and the sergeant left by the front door. The officers sat down.

"Major, I hope you knew I was coming. My orders were in Lubbock, and I assume you also received yours from Washington."

"Yes, yes I did." He opened a box and held it

out. "Cigar, Colonel McCoy?"

Spur took one, it was short and thicker than he liked. He knew it would be mild without the usual bite of his favorite black twisted cigars. They went through the ritual of snipping off the end of the stogies and lighting them.

Major Donaldson leaned back and blew out a mouthful of smoke.

"Sir, my orders originally called for me to furnish you with a detachment of ten mounted men to serve as an escort to Roswell and on to the Rio Grande. I was prepared to do so. Then yesterday a rider came through from San Antonio. That's the U.S. Army's Department of Texas headquarters, as you know.

"Colonel Zackery there has instructed me to cease at once furnishing or providing any kind of escort service through Apache country, especially the Mescalero lands and the Chiricahua country."

Spur leaned forward, eyes hooded, his face showing surprise and anger. "There must be some mistake, Major Donaldson. Were not my orders signed by Major General Wilton D. Halleck?"

Donaldson stood and walked around the room.

"Yes, Colonel, they were, and he outranks my boss Colonel Zackery. However we have a problem of timing. The date on the telegram detailing my orders concerning you and the escort, that was forwarded by mail, was over three weeks ago. My orders from San Antonio are dated six days ago. The rider came in late last night."

"Ten men and a non-com, Major. Surely you can spare us that many men."

"Specific orders to the contrary, Colonel. As

you know, orders that come through regular Army channels always take precedent over casual orders and requests. What would you do in my place, Colonel?"

"I would indicate to my superiors that the current order did not arrive until after the ten men left to safeguard my party. You do know that I have seven nuns and a priest who insist on making the trip?"

Major Donaldson nodded.

"They threatened to go without me, if I refused to take them. I can't believe that you would let us cross without an escort. Weren't two wagon loads of civilians massacred last week out there?"

"Yes, our burial detail had to function after the raid. Six men, seven women and four children, all dead."

"Major, we've both been in the Army long enough to know that there are ways around and through any order."

"Colonel, I didn't tell you all of my communication from my headquarters. Word has been received of a general uprising of the Apache renegades now in the Mescalero and Chiricahua tribal zones. This post is to brace itself for a possible external attack, and to send out patrols on a daily basis reaching up to twenty miles into hostile territory to show the flag and to watch for any Indian movements."

"Almost a state of war."

"Still a state of war with the Indians, Colonel."

"But we can pass through, without your aid?"

"I was surprised the orders did not indicate

that we should stop all traveling between here and Roswell. That order might come at any time. I suggest you turn around and wait in Lubbock."

"That's what I told the ladies, but you don't know Mother Superior Mary Benedict."

The major sat down and Spur stood and paced. He was checkmated at every turn. He knew the army. Major Donaldson was right, he had to obey his immediate superior. Halleck's orders did not go through channels, and were secondary. He turned toward the door.

"Major, my compliments to your colonel. We'll be pushing on for Roswell. I hope we don't cause any extra work for your burial detail."

He went out the door without waiting for a reply. His horse was tied outside. Spur mounted up and rode. He would ask once more that they return. He would try to get Chiquita on his side.

A half hour later he pulled up with Chiquita, where Mother Benedict had stopped the mules. The three outriders came in and they talked. Spur presented the situation bluntly.

"So that means no army escort. Not one soldier will ride shotgun for us. It leaves us no option, we have to turn around and wait out the order in Lubbock. I'll send a letter to the nearest telegraph office and try to get authorization through the San Antonio Army headquarters."

"And how long will that take?" Mother Benedict asked.

"Two, maybe three weeks. If we had a telegraph in town it would be a matter of two or three days."

The Mother Superior looked at Chiquita. "You told me you're half Mescalero. Do you know your people well enough so that we can sneak through, get past them without having to fight them?"

"Most of them, Mother. Nobody, not even another Apache can sneak past all the Mescaleros. That means a wagon can't do it either. We can go around or in back of most of them."

"But one band of ten Mescalero braves would turn us into live targets. We would be little more than hunting practice for them," Spur said.

"Maybe, maybe not," Chiquita countered.

The three stared at one another.

Spur snapped his reins and wished he could swear for five minutes. He looked at Chiquita, then at the nun. "Mother Superior, you are responsible for eight lives, eight Catholic church worker lives. From a practical standpoint, I don't see how you can vote to go across. I'm casting my vote against making the trip."

The white strip over Mother Superior's tanned face was already showing a pink tinge. She frowned and rubbed her forehead, then closed her eyes and clasped the cross that hung just inside her blue shirt. She sighed.

"I vote to cross, to continue," Mother Superior Benedict said.

She and Spur looked at Chiquita.

"I am half Mescalero. I know the country. I know the good spirits. Look!" She pointed upward and they stared into the blue sky and saw a swooping split wing hawk, gliding around and around on a rising current of air.

"When the crooked nosed hawk rises on the wind, all will be well. It is Mescalero. I say that we go forward."

"Damn!" Spur said. He turned his bay,

slapped her flanks with the reins and galloped two hundred yards into the country, stopped and stared at the sky. He turned the reddish brown mare around and walked her back to the wagon. Spur got off his horse and pulled a shovel from where it had been fastened on the side of the Conestoga box for ready use.

He showed it to the women.

"Do you know what this is?" he shouted. Before they could answer he dug a spadful of earth and flung it away from them.

"This is a shovel, and if you insist on making the trip against my recommendation, and against that of Major Donaldson of the United States Army, then this shovel will be used often. To bury our dead before we get to Roswell!"

Spur marched back to the wagon, secured the shovel where it had been before and walked to his bay.

He mounted and glared at both women.

Both returned his stare calmly.

"We continue," Mother Superior said.

"We continue," Chiquita echoed.

The middle-aged nun on the wagon seat briskly slapped the reins on the mules' backs and the Conestoga rolled forward.

Chiquita, smiling at Spur, swung her horse around and moved in front of the wagon, taking the lead.

Spur McCoy, mother hen to eight little chicks and one dragon, scowled and watched the wagon moving westward.

When it was about fifty yards away, he took off his hat, wiped the sweat from his forehead, then reset the low crowned Stetson, still scowling, and rode after them.

SEVEN

Spur caught up with the Conestoga and two nuns riding next to the rig. He turned a stern face toward the Mother Superior. He tipped his hat and then rode in closer.

"Mother Benedict, remember what the store-keeper said about your nuns? That it would be kinder to line them up in the city and shoot them. Remember that, the man was serious. We are moving into a life and death situation. How well we can do what we must do, will determine how many of us are alive to ride into Roswell."

"The Lord will protect us, and we'll do everything we can to protect ourselves," she said.

"Good. On our noontime stop there will be required rifle instructions for everyone, including Clark and you. Be sure your whiskey priest is sober enough to learn something about these Spencer repeating rifles." Before the nun could respond Spur wheeled his horse and galloped forward toward the slight figure on the roan gelding a quarter of a mile along a slight downslope.

71

When he came up to Chiquita, she had dismounted and was sitting on the ground, her legs folded, her arms outthrust as she stared at the cloudless sky.

He dropped from the horse and waited.

She remained in that position for another two minutes, then turned and stared at him.

"I know, Chiquita, the Indian spirits are everywhere. Go to it, anything might help. Right now I'd take a Shaman if I could find one and use him as scout."

"You are right, roundeye. The Indian spirits are all around us, in the rivers, the trees, the broad plateaus, the parched mountains. They are in every animal from the ant to the buffalo and in this seven dog I ride. I would not expect a roundeye to understand or even appreciate.

"The spirits bring us either success or failure, make the game run near us for a kill, heal the sick, guarantee fertility. The spirits watch over the welfare of all Mescaleros, everywhere."

"Even a Breed?"

"Especially, because I also have a St. Christopher's medal with me."

"You know this is a fool's mission. It could become a total disaster, a tragedy."

"Not with Chiquita as your guide. Remember, I, too, am Mescalero!"

"A Mescalero arrow or .52 caliber rifle slug will slam into your flesh just as easily as into one of the roundeye Catholics back there. Do you realize you have seven women and a drunkard in that wagon? They know nothing of the high desert, nothing of how to defend themselves. And none of them have ever raised a hand in violence. Not very good troops.''

"But Mother Superior is determined, that makes up for a lot.'' She pointed ahead to the west. "See the thin line of green? A small river. One of the last we will see for some time. We must refill our water barrels there. We need to make fifteen miles today.''

"I'd guess you will swing to the south so we miss most of the better hunting grounds of the Mescaleros?''

"How did you . . .'' She looked up and she nodded. "You must know more of the Mescalero and this country than I thought. You've been here before.''

"And survived, which could be more than I'll do this time. The deeper we get into Mescalero country, the more we must consider moving at night and sleeping during the day. Do you agree?''

"The third day will be our last travel in the sunlight.'' A new appreciation for him showed in her eyes. "This roundeye may be useful yet on our dangerous journey,'' she said, a small smile showing. Then she rose, leaped on the back of her horse and rode ahead.

Spur wheeled and walked his mount toward the wagon. He tied his bay on a lead rope and swung up to the back of the wagon. Two sisters were altering pants. One of them was Teresa. She smiled and now he could see her short blonde hair again.

"Sisters, I need to get a box and do some work with it. Is there room?''

Sister Mary Ruth said she wanted to ride up front with Mother.

Spur found what he was hunting and sat down on another box and took out the Spencer rifle tubular magazines. He began loading seven of the big .52 caliber rounds into each of the tubes.

"What are those?" Teresa asked.

"Magazine tubes for the rifles," he said, looking up. Then he couldn't help staring at her. He glanced around. "Do you know how surprised I was when I saw you?"

Sister Teresa laughed softly. "I have some idea. I haven't been a nun very long. I . . . I just had to break out of the order for a few hours."

"You certainly did that." Spur went back to loading the tubes. If they got hit by Mescaleros they would have a supply of the loaded tubes ready to go. He wanted ten tubes for each rifle, but they didn't have that many back at the store. He remembered buying four of the boxes with ten tubes in each box.

"Can I help?" Teresa asked.

He showed her how to load the shells, pushing each one in the tube against the pressure of the spring. She caught on at once and soon was loading them as quickly as he did.

"You'll get a chance to use these this noon," he said. "We're having basic rifle training. I have a gut feeling we're all going to need to know how to shoot the Spencers before this trip is over."

"I don't know anything about guns," Teresa said.

"You will before nightfall."

She let her hand brush his leg and he looked at her sharply. She pulled the hand back and continued loading the rounds.

"Seemed like a good idea," she said and smiled again.

They were over half done. Spur eased to the tailgate and jumped out. He walked along behind the tailgate watching her.

"Finish up on these, would you please? I have to check up ahead and see if there's a place to stop for dinner."

Spur felt a relief when he stepped into his saddle and rode. Teresa could be a problem, but not if he didn't let her. She was looking for more loving, but it was impossible. Not even Father Clark would hump a nun in a situation like this. Spur snorted and changed his mind. Clark would try for any female within reach, and he was sure the Mother Superior had warned all her nuns about him.

He rode forward a quarter of a mile in front of the wagon. The trail, such as it was, showed faint and often became non-existent. It made little difference since west was the direction, and the flat land with only a few streams, could be crossed at almost any point. Now and then they saw wheel tracks pounded into the earth when it had been much softer than it was now.

McCoy could not see the scout, Chiquita. He wondered where she was. He paused for a moment on the big bay mare and scanned the land ahead. He'd heard that on a level place you could see only seven miles in any direction. Beyond that the curvature of the earth sent your line of sight out into space.

Nowhere in the next seven miles could he see the line of green that he and Chiquita had spotted before from the small rise. Fortunes of travel. They would stop within an hour wherever they happened to be. They did not need a stream, although the animals would want water by nightfall. They would have to wait until mid afternoon at least and the small stream and the splotch of green he had seen.

Spur rode back to the wagon, tied his mount and climbed up on the front bench. The white stripe across Mother Benedict's forehead had turned from bright pink to boisterous red.

He took off his hat and eased it on the nun's head.

"I'm burning?"

"Yes. We forgot to buy you hats. Sunbonnets would be a help. Can one of your ladies sew up some?"

"Yes, we'll use cloth from one of the habits. That's a fine idea, Mr. McCoy."

He took the reins while Mother Benedict swiveled around and climbed in through the front of the covered wagon and called to the sisters in back.

An hour later they stopped on the raw prairie of the high plateau of Western Texas. Sister Maria had been designated as cook and she fried up bacon and eggs as a treat. They would use them up today and tomorrow before they spoiled.

Spur got out the seven Spencers and checked them over. He found a large rock about thirty yards away that he used as a target and loaded each of the Spencers then shot a round through each weapon.

Three of the nuns watched him.

"Ladies, now is as good a time as any." He

positioned the three ten yards from the wagon facing outward and had them sit on the ground. He stood in front of them with a Spencer.

"Ladies, this is a Spencer repeating rifle. It will fire seven times without reloading. It fires a .52 caliber slug from a number fifty-six spencer rim fire cartridge. The barrel is round and thirty inches long and rifled with three broad grooves. The rifling makes the bullet spin so it travels straight once it leaves the barrel."

He moved his hand to the rear sight. "This is the sliding rear sight, and up here is the blade front sight. The total length of this weapon is forty-seven inches and it weighs a little more than ten pounds."

He unlocked the magazine and drew it out of the butt of the rifle. "The rounds in this tube load through the base plate, then lock in place. When it's empty you open it, take out the used tubes and put in a loaded one. The spent brass fly out of the breach of the weapon. Have any of you fired a rifle before?"

One had, Sister Mary Francis. Spur handed her a Spencer.

"Sister, lift your knees to rest your elbows on, then sight it on that rock out there and fire."

She took the rifle and looked up, surprised. "It's so heavy!"

"You'll get used to it. Try a shot."

She lifted the rifle, braced her elbows on her knees and fired. Dust spurted up twenty yards beyond the rock. The two other nuns laughed. The kick of the heavy round slammed the rifle into her shoulder.

"Try it again."

This time the round hit twenty feet in front of them. Spur frowned, then went to the wagon and brought back a wooden box.

"Rest the rifle on this and try it again."

She did. This time she hit the rock. He had her fire until the seven shots were gone. Then he talked her through taking out the empty tube and putting in a new one.

One by one he trained the nuns in how to use the Spencer.

They took a break for a trail dinner, the bacon and fried eggs and some baked bread they had brought from the town's small bakery. Any bread after that would have to be fresh baked biscuits.

As the ammo tubes emptied, Sister Teresa refilled them.

Spur thanked her. "Yes, we should keep the forty tubes filled at all times. We never know when we might need them." He showed everyone where the tubes would be stored. The rifles were at several locations around the wagon for quick use. Four loaded tubes were with each Spencer.

At first Mother Superior Benedict backed away from the weapons training.

Spur spoke softly to her. "Sister, you got us into this mess, and you might have to help hold off a few dozen Mescaleros. I suggest you learn how to shoot extremely well. Your very life may depend on it. This would be a ridiculous, senseless way to die, proving nothing, certainly not a fitting ending to your service to your church."

She watched Spur for a moment. Then took the Spencer, hefted it a moment and standing up put all seven of the rounds in the center of the rock.

The nuns cheered.

"I was raised on a farm before I went into the order," she said.

Father Clark came late to the meal. He took one bite of the fried eggs, rushed to one side and threw up. Mother Benedict vanished inside the wagon and a few moments later Spur saw her pouring what was left of a pint of whiskey into the dirt. She threw the bottle as far as she could.

They did not take the usual two hour dinner break of a normal wagon train. Instead they pushed forward. By three that afternoon they could see the green band of trees near the stream and by four-thirty they pulled in and stopped in the shade.

Chiquita told Spur this was the best place to camp for five miles ahead. They had covered almost twelve miles.

"We'll camp here tonight," Spur told them. Then he found Sister Cecilia, the other farm girl, and helped her unhitch the mules. She was a tall woman, about thirty and could handle the hitching and harnessing. They pulled off the harness and tethered the mules in some knee high grass after giving them a good long drink.

When all the horses were also cared for, they began to gather wood for a small cooking fire. Three of the nuns took off shoes and stockings, rolled up their pant legs a few inches and dangled their feet in the cool, clear water of the stream. It was no more than a foot deep and perhaps fifteen feet wide. After the day's dry, hot ride it was a practical oasis.

Supper came just as it began to get dark. Sister Mary Ruth had put a five gallon crock full of beans to soak. She would cook them at breakfast and again at noon. Supper was beef jerky and bread, with plenty of dried apricots and hot coffee.

Spur had seen Chiquita ride off just after they stopped. She came back at full dark, had some food and talked to Spur.

"I found some signs up river. Two or three Mescaleros were here hunting, rabbits probably. They made a small kill and left two days ago, moving west and north. We should not be bothered by them. That was the only sign I saw of any of my people."

"That phrase worries me a little, Chiquita. You said *my people*. Will that make a difference if the Mescaleros attack us? Can you shoot down your people?"

"Spur McCoy. Know that I am Mexican by choice, Indian by accident. I have chosen the roundeye way of life, not the Mescalero. The Apache, and especially the Mescalero, raid and kill for pleasure. War is the Apache's vocation, they glory in it. The Mescaleros are honest but cruel, treacherous killers who torture their captives. I was raised by nuns in a softer, more human atmosphere.

"Yes, Mr. McCoy. I can and I will defend my charges, and my own life with every skill and power that I have. They are *my people* only by chance, not by choice."

"Good, which guard duty do you want, dark or midnight, or midnight to five A.M.?"

"The early morning hours are most

dangerous, I'll take them," she said. Chiquita finished her food. "I'll be by the golden cottonwood, wake me at twelve."

She took her blanket to the cottonwood and was soon sleeping.

After the meal the small camp quieted. The nuns were bone weary after the first day. Father Clark appeared for only a short time to eat, then went back to the wagon. Spur knew that by tomorrow he would be bone dry, desperately sober, hung over and hurting. Then Spur would start turning up the pressure on Clark, and get him functioning and helping them. As much as McCoy disliked the idea, Clark would have to help them in a tight situation. He would need some rifle training first.

Spur saw Mother Superior bed down her charges. They were on the ground in blankets, with their feet to the fire. They slept in twos, close together, touching for security. Then Mother Superior went back to the front of the wagon where she had built a small nest of her own.

McCoy established a perimeter guard trail, and walked it one way and then the other. He hunkered down next to a clump of brush and listened. There was almost no sound. A night hawk called now and then. He heard the beating of the wings of a big owl which quieted when the huge bird soared from one tree to another. The sound of nothing beat at his ears, creating a soft rushing.

His evaluation of the day was quick and simple.

So far, so good.

It was what lay ahead that worried him. The deeper they plunged into Mescalero country, the more apt they were to run into a band of Mescaleros or to be seen by a hunting party or a wandering scout.

Then the fun would begin. Then people would start dying. An attack by Mescaleros would not be a massive horse charge. The Mescaleros seldom used horses. They were more apt to eat a horse if they could catch one, rather than ride it. They could run all day through the high desert, and usually outdistance a man on horseback.

A Mescalero brave moved through the land like a wolf or coyote, taking advantage of cover and the terrain.

If they attacked it would be suddenly, with deadly surprise. When they were out maneuvered, or out gunned, they simply melted away into the plains or plateaus or hills and were not seen again.

That was the Mescalero way, the killing way, the ages old way of death.

Ever vigilant was the key. Now there was little danger. The Mescaleros almost never fought or attacked at night. If they had spotted the lone wagon, they would rest now and ready a welcome for them shortly after daylight.

At midnight he woke Chiquita with a touch on her shoulder. Before he could pull back his hand a sharp knife lay against it and round black eyes stared up at him.

"Don't ever touch me!" she said sharply. "A word or two will wake me. Stay out of reach of my blade."

"Good morning to you, too, Chiquita. Nothing

is stirring. Time for me to get some sleep." Spur moved away, not watching her rise or to see where she went. She would do it right, she was a hired scout, and she was Mescalero.

He rolled up in his blankets, looked over at the six sleeping nuns and wondered which one was Teresa. He snorted, turned over and went to sleep.

EIGHT

The missionaries were all sore, stiff and complaining in the morning. Father Clark answered the breakfast call and looked half dead. His hangover was still pounding at him. He growled at the nuns until Mother Superior Benedict had a quiet word with him. Then he took his bacon and cooked dried prunes and sat by himself on the ground, eating and glaring at everyone.

Spur helped Sister Cecilia with the harness for the mules. She remembered her farm days and learned quickly. She would be able to do it by herself from now on.

They hit the trail at slightly before six A.M. while the touches of light were breaking apart the solid black of the east behind them.

The three nuns who had not ridden the horses the first day got to ride today. They were far from expert, but could ride well enough to stay up with the plodding mules. Teresa was the best rider of the group.

Chiquita talked briefly with Spur over her breakfast.

"Yes, here we swing more to the south, as you guessed. We go around two water holes, but we will have more than enough water for two days. At that time we will come to Agua Caliente. There are some warm springs there but the water is not sulpur so it is fit to drink. Few Mescaleros travel that far south this time of year to hunt."

"Nothing for the stock to drink after this morning?" Spur asked.

"Late in the day there should be a small stream that has not yet dried up for the summer."

"Our animals hope so."

"I may not be back until noon. Southwest until midday and we should be right. I'll find you." She put down her tin plate and fork.

"Hey, so far so good," Spur said. "What are our chances of getting through unseen?"

"About a hundred to one." She shook her pretty face sending the braid bouncing behind her. Dark eyes shaded even deeper purple black. "No, worse than that. No chance at all. The Mescals are hunting meat. Do you know how long a tribe of twenty-five can live off one mule?"

"Best hunting this time of year is the seven-dog and whatever roundeyes happen to be along for the walk. How did the Mescaleros ever call the horse seven-dog?"

"We used to use big dogs to pull sleds and made packs for them. They could carry about sixty pounds. When the horse came along the Mescaleros decided a horse could carry seven times as much as a dog, so . . . seven-dog."

"Makes sense."

She looked at him sternly. "We are going to have much trouble before this trip is over. But it may be well that you are along. You are not the worst roundeye I have ever met." She let the smallest trace of a smile touch her serious face, then she stood in an easy move and ran to her horse. A moment later she had mounted and was gone. There was not even a canteen on her saddle.

Spur dug into the supplies and found the canteens, and made sure each of the riding horses had a filled water bottle hung over the pommel. A precaution.

The little band moved slowly across the prairie of the great plateau. They were still in Texas since it was sixty-five miles as the crow flies to get to the New Mexican line. With the wandering route any wagon must take, it would probably be five days before they reached the state line.

In places the spring grass had not yet turned brown. It rose in undulating waves across the wide expanses of land, looking sometimes more like a sea than a landmass. In places the soil had given up the last of the spring moisture and the grass was a rich golden color, turning a square mile at a time into a prospector's fantasy.

The Conestoga rolled on. Spur was glad he had settled on the sturdy wagon. So far they had experienced no trouble with it and the mules were pulling a relatively light load for the four of them. He hoped that would mean no mechanical problems with the rig.

As they angled southwest they followed a

gentle depression that began a valley here but was never more than ten or twelve feet below the rest of the land's contour. The small wet weather stream had long since evaporated into the sand, but here and there they saw a damp spot. They were nothing worthy of the word spring that could be used.

Half a mile farther down Mother Superior made her first driving mistake. She elected to go through one such wet area, rather than drive fifty yards around it.

The mules sank in past their hocks into the dampness and the front wheels dropped in a foot deep, but the mules, now on firm footing beyond the sink, pulled the front wheels through. The wider rimmed rear wheels would have no trouble in the soft mud, Spur hoped. He was on the verge of shouting at Mother Benedict to whip the mules for more power.

Too late. The rear wheels with the most weight on them quickly sank to the axle and the mules pawed the ground. The big Conestoga was securely stuck in the mud in the middle of a semi desert.

"Everybody out!" Spur bellowed. The nuns scrambled out, then slowly the priest exited.

Spur stared at the sink. It was barely six feet wide. Already the front wheels were on dry ground. He hated the idea of unloading the whole wagon and levering it out. Instead he called to the nuns riding the horses. Using ropes they hitched the four riding horses to the singletree the first team was fronted by.

The ropes went around the singletree and then around the saddle horn of each mount.

Spur looked over all the knots, then at the women.

"When I give the signal, we all ride ahead and pull that wagon right out of the mud. Everyone ready?"

Heads nodded. Behind, Mother Superior Benedict took off her sunbonnet and wiped her brow. Then she said she was prepared.

"Ready . . . Go!" Spur shouted.

The four mules and four horses strained against the leather and the ropes. Slowly the rear wheels began to move, an inch, then a foot, then one of the mules slipped and fell in the traces and all progress stopped.

Spur dismounted and went back to the mule. He urged the animal to stand, then stroked his ears and the side of his neck. A final pat on the mule calmed it and Spur went back to his saddle.

"Progress, we're making progress. Let's do it again. Ready . . . Go!"

This time the wagon refused to move for a moment, then it inched ahead, slowed and then in one burst slid forward and rolled out of the muck to the dry land.

Everyone cheered.

They paused for five minutes while Spur checked out the wagon. The undercarriage was mudded, but it would dry, the mud harden and fall off within a few miles.

Mother Superior had stepped to the ground to look over the rig as well. She glanced at Spur now and smiled.

"I know. Next time if I have any question about the footing, I should drive around it. I'll remember. But you get to drive when we have to ford the first river we come to."

"That won't be much of a problem. We might touch the headwaters of the Sulphur Draw stream, but up here it won't be more than a creek. Then we'll see how much water the Pecos has in it."

They rolled again. By noontime Spur figured with the early start and lack of trouble that they had covered a little over eight miles.

Chiquita had not returned. They stopped on a slight rise so she could find them and ate biscuits and baked beans for lunch. The beans were not quite done, but could be eaten. They would be cooked for as long as the noon break lasted, then cooked the final time at the supper stop. They were laced with the ever present bacon.

The way the bacon was smoked and cured it would last even in the heat for three to four weeks, and quickly became the meat staple. Some wagons carried along a chicken coop, to produce eggs and a cow for milk. Larger units herded a dozen steers along the route, killing one a week to provide meat for fifty to a hundred people for two days before it turned rancid. Salt pork also was a staple for wagoners, but for a two week trip, Spur had elected not to bring any.

Chiquita came back just as they were packing up. Ruth provided her with a tin plate of food and a large cup of coffee and biscuits.

She brought with her two large jackrabbits she had shot, but not with her rifle. On her saddle hung a newly made bow and two arrows.

"A Mescalero is not worthy of the name if she can't make a bow and arrow in the hunting grounds," she told them. "We are now deep enough into Mescalero country so we should not fire our weapons unless we must. A rifle shot can be heard out here for twenty miles if the wind is right."

She gave the rabbits to Sister Cecilia who deftly butchered and skinned them and put the slender carcasses in a big pot filled with salt water. They both would be roasted for supper.

Soon they were moving again. Chiquita told Spur there was another small stream half a day's ride ahead. They could get to it by driving the wagon until nearly dark.

"Any more sign?"

"No, not here, they must be staying to the north. Our luck may be holding."

Spur laughed and pointed at her. "Or our spirits are with us on this trip."

"Do not make fun of something you don't understand," Chiquita said sharply. "You are a roundeye."

"Which means I can't understand anything Indian?" Spur asked quickly. "I know when a person has been rejected by both her cultures that it must hurt terribly. I know that a woman needs more than a horse and a .44 and a job so she can make an honest living. I know a lot about you, Chiquita."

Her black eyes watched his for several seconds. Neither of them looked away. At last her face curved into a real smile. "I hope you do know me, gringo. Then you will know what I am going to do when we have a fight with the

Mescals. You will know my tactics and I yours.
It will help us defeat the Mescals and that way
we both will live longer." She rode rapidly away
for a hundred yards, then came back letting her
horse walk.

"There is a soft place ahead we must cross, no
way around it. A seep of some sort and probably
the last one. See how the land becomes more dry
with every mile? Caution Mother to be careful at
the wet spot."

"We'll get through."

"I'm going to probe to the north, see what I
can find. I'll leave the horse on a lead rope
behind the wagon. This is Mascalero work, the
seven-dog would only get in my way and attract
attention. A wolf or a coyote is harder to see
than a horse." She rode to the wagon, tied the
horse and trotted away to the north, her newly
made bow and three arrows in her left hand,
where any good Mescalero hunter would carry
them.

Spur McCoy watched her go. If there were any
Mescals within five miles of their route, she
would spot them, stay unseen and return to
warn him.

He sat on his mount and dug out a crooked
black cheroot and lit it with a stinker match.
The smoke was bitter and biting and he blew it
out. At least he had chosen the scout well for
this ill conceived and ill advised trip. If they
made it to Roswell, New Mexico, they would
owe it mostly to the skill and knowledge of that
small Mexican-Indian Breed jogging into the
distance. Today she wore tan pants and a tan
blouse almost the same color.

Even at a hundred yards he had trouble finding her as she blended into the combination of prairie grass and more and more bare patches of thin sandy soil.

Spur told Mother Benedict about the soft spot ahead, then rode forward to find it. Teresa rode a way with him, but he sent her back.

"Teresa, you know we can't ride off alone," Spur said with a sudden anger. "Our first job is to get across to Roswell."

"My first job is to show you how well I can make love. You'll see." She turned, her sunbonnet shading her face, and rode back to the wagon.

Spur found the soft place and waited. It was an almost stream that oozed and puddled for five miles across a traversing gradual slope. He walked his bay into it and she sank in to her hocks but then the ground seemed to hold. He worked across the twenty yard width of the soggy ground but found no real problem until near the far side. There it turned into a real sink which could probably swallow up the mules and wagon and not leave a trace.

He moved to the left and tried again. After another half hour of trial and error he found the end of the sink, and marked a safe route across with sticks.

When the wagon arrived, Father Clark rode one of the horses. He had been on a mount before. He saw the sticks, guided Mother Benedict along the path and led her safely through to the other side.

The nuns in the wagon cheered, and the other two nuns on horseback followed the wagon through the same path.

Father Clark rode up to Spur and scowled at him.

"I know we have to put up with each other for a few more days out here. I also know that you don't like me. I'm not telling anyone you are my favorite cowboy either. Don't worry, I can ride and shoot. I was in the army during the war, the Gray, naturally. When we're in Roswell, we will have a settling of accounts."

"We may," Spur said. "If you're a priest again by then, you won't have any trouble from me."

"So? You may still very well have some trouble from me." Father Clark stared past a long, slightly reddish nose at Spur, said nothing more and swung back toward the wagon.

The sun came down hotter than it had been the first day. Spur pulled the kerchief around his neck up to cover half of his face as they rode forward. Sweat ran down his hair and dripped on his neck.

He slashed away the moisture under his hat brim and resettled the Stetson. It was going to be over ninety degrees that day.

Spur was half asleep in his saddle when he heard a scream behind him thirty yards. He came alert at once, spun the bay around, his hand on his .45.

The big wagon sat at an odd angle. The mules had stopped, and Spur saw that the left front Conestoga wheel had dropped into a hole and splintered three spokes.

There was not a chance they were going to make the next water before dark now. He rode back to the wagon, remembering the joys of changing a wagon wheel on a heavily loaded rig —especially with only one other man to help him.

NINE

Spur, Father Clark, and all the nuns had been working hard for almost an hour. The mules had been unhitched and the wagon tongue removed, then several wooden boxes had been brought from the wagon to form a fulcrum. The boxes had been placed just outside of the wagon box near the front end of the rig.

Spur and Father Clark carried the wagon tongue to the fulcrum, placed the heavy end of it on the box and then tilted it downward until it would slip under the wagon frame.

Spur pushed it under the wagon box a foot and waved his arms.

"All right, the hard work is done. Let's rest a minute." He slumped on the box, panting. The temperature was still climbing. He figured it was nearing a hundred degrees. "Do you ladies have that wire loosened up on the spare wheel?" he asked.

A variety of answers came back. He heaved to his feet and went around the box to check the wheel wired to the undercarriage of the wagon.

It was loosened. He moved the nuns back, snipped one wire with the side cutter pliers and let that side of the wheel down to the ground, then cut the other side. He slid the wheel out and positioned it next to the wagon.

"Now comes the part that takes lots of brain power. We all jump on the wagon tongue and hope we weigh enough to lift the wagon up with our basic machine lever here. Hang on to the tongue, sit on it, lay on it. Anything to boost up the axle so we can push some more wooden boxes under it. Let's give it a try."

He caught the tongue that was slanting six feet into the air and pulled it down so the nuns could grab it. Then they jumped on it bringing it lower and lower and the wagon box higher.

Spur let go and hurried to the front of the wagon. Father Clark had pushed a second box under the axle. They needed another foot. Spur found three timbers, four by fours and placed them on top of the wooden box under the axle, then put the last one on top of those and it was high enough.

The nuns let the wagon tongue down slowly and the wooden boxes under the wagon held.

"Now, all we have to do is pull this wheel off, throw it away and put on the new one," Spur said. "Then pray that we don't break another one."

With the pressure off the wheel it came free in a few minutes and the new one was rolled on and pinned into place. They hoisted the wagon box once more with the lever so the men could take out the blocking under the axle and let the box down slowly. The wheel hit the ground and held.

A tired cheer went up.

Another half hour and the boxes had been stowed back in the wagon, the tongue put back in place and the mules hitched up. They would be too late to get to the patch of greenery before dark that they could see some four or five miles ahead.

Spur pushed them along, but called a halt a half hour before dusk. They had brought firewood with them from the last stop as a precaution. They needed it. There were no trees not even any brush here. The tall grass had given way to stunted growth and a small bush now and again. They were coming more into a desert area of lower rainfall.

Chiquita walked into the camp just as it grew dark. She looked tired. She at once took over roasting the two rabbits over an open fire. She let the flames burn down to glowing coals and lowered a spit until the meat was two inches from the heat, then turned them slowly.

Soon fat sizzled in the coals and the meat cooked. It was the best meal they had eaten since leaving Lubbock. Roast rabbit, well done baked beans, biscuits and dried apples for desert and plenty of strong, black coffee.

Spur talked to Chiquita as they ate.

"Find any friends?" he asked.

"No signs at all. No more game, either. There should be no Mescals hunting this area because there's nothing here to hunt. The raiders should be working the regular route across to Roswell. We should be about ten miles south of that."

"Good. Let's hope your spirit friends, and my Irish luck stays with us. I'll take both watches tonight. You need some sleep."

"No. I do my job. You take the first watch as usual. I'm going to sleep over on that side." She pointed to the north just off the firelight. Spur took his tin plate and cup back to the pot of hot water and washed them, got a second cup of coffee and walked around the tethered horses and the six mules.

For a moment he wondered if they should have brought extra harness for the spare mules? It would have come in handy to pull the wagon out of the sink. Without the harness for the mules he had to rely on the saddle horses.

McCoy dismissed it and concentrated on walking around the little camp. The wagon shielded the fire so it showed only to the south. Couldn't be too careful. Only one more day of traveling in the daytime? Night movement with a wagon would be slow and dangerous. He would have another talk with Chiquita about it.

He watched the camp fire burn down. Sleeping had been no problem for any of them. The nuns were used to working, but this was a different kind of labor. There had been far fewer problems with Father Clark than Spur had figured. Perhaps he only went on occasional flings with the whores and John Barleycorn. Perhaps.

The fire went out. He saw the six sleeping forms near the embers. Mother Superior and the priest still shared different ends of the wagon at night. Chiquita was a small curled ball between the fire and the horses and mules.

Spur stood and looked out as a half moon rode into the sky. Not a cloud. The stars sparkled and winked at him.

Not a sound. No wind, no birds calling out here.

Then a solitary coyote howled in the distance. He listened. An answering call came from the other way. Then a third and a fourth. For ten minutes there was a chorus of coyotes serenading to each other. It was some crude form of communication, and probably part of the mating rituals. The calls were higher pitched but not as complex as those of wolves.

A pack of wolves howling up a chorus could run chills along a grown man's spine. The calls of the coyotes seemed more of a serenade than of signalling any danger. Coyotes were afraid of humans. The only one he had ever see even try to attack a human was a large male that had rabies. The animal had been actually foaming at the mouth before he was shot dead in a small town in Kansas.

Spur watched the Big Dipper climb in the sky. It was on its nightly journey of making nearly a complete circle around the North Star. By watching the position of the Big Dipper any cowhand worth his beans and bacon knew what time it was to within ten minutes.

When the Big Dipper told Spur it was one A.M., he went and called softly to Chiquita. She came awake at once, the knife already in her hand. She looked at the sky.

"Why did you let me sleep an extra hour?"

"Because I'm bigger than you are, and I'm tougher than you are, but most important, because I'm your boss. Any questions?"

She smiled, checked her .44 and folded her blankets.

"Quiet?"

"Yes."

"Anything?"

"Not even a nightbird. We did have some coyotes serenading us, but they are either paired up for the night or sleeping."

She shot him a quick look, then waved in the thin moonlight and walked toward the wagon and a drink of coffee from the pot that still sat on the now cold coals.

Spur took his blankets from the back of the wagon and lay down in a slight depression twenty yards from the fire. He stared at the stars for a moment, then turned on his side and cushioned his head with his arms. His eyes had begun to get heavy when he was aware of someone near him. He tensed, his hand holding the .45 under the blankets.

"Be quiet, Spur McCoy and I won't scream," a soft woman's voice said.

He opened his eyes and saw Teresa's beautiful face staring at him from her blanket beside him.

"I thought we might share our covers . . . so we could stay warmer," Teresa said. She folded back the heavy cloth and in the moonlight he saw her white body, naked against the darkness.

"Teresa!" he whispered. "I told you . . ."

Then she had pushed on top of him and pressed her mouth over his. The kiss had begun as an attack to quiet him, but soon the intensity wavered and it became softer, more pliable, more seductive, and then it was a plea, a whimper of desire that Spur could not ignore.

Spur was angry at first, but as the kiss continued and he felt her body against his, he remembered how she set him on fire back in Lubbock, and he opened his mouth for her tongue to slant into him.

A moment later he had pulled the blanket over her and his hands found her breasts. Teresa was panting as she unfastened the buttons on his pants.

"Don't even take them off!" She whispered. "I want it rough and sudden and hard! Take me right now before I even get ready! Be rough with me this time."

She rolled on her back and pulled him over her. His weapon was cocked and ready and she lifted her parted knees and he lanced into her waiting slot with a suddenness that left her gasping for air, moaning in delight with touches of pain. Then she wrapped her legs around his waist as he lifted a little off her chest and pounded into her.

For the moment pure lust commanded him. Spur McCoy was a sexual animal craving satisfaction. He hammered at her and she rose to meet each powering thrust. Her breasts heaved and her face worked as she surged into a climax of her own.

Spur barely noticed. Again and again he slammed his hips against hers until his pelvic bone hurt with each plunge. Then the trigger opened the valves and closed others and his seed blasted deeply into her and he heaved and panted again, then for a long moment he lay, locked inside of her.

"Wonderful, sweetheart!" she cooed into his ear in a whisper. "We have all night. Cecilia is my sleep partner. She never wakes up, and she snores. We're safe.''

He lay there a moment more, then slid away and lay beside her.

"Don't worry about my being a nun. I'm really not a nun. My father made me join the order. I'm still a novice. My father caught me in bed at home with two boys. Evidently he watched a while before he came crashing in. He said I had to join the convent or a brothel. As soon as we get to Roswell I'm renouncing my vows and staying there.''

"I'm a little relieved to hear that, Teresa. But we have to be quiet, Chiquita could be watching us.''

"Too bad,'' Teresa whispered. "Let her find her own man.'' She reached under the blanket to his crotch.

They both laughed softly, put their heads under the blanket and talked, then made love again. Spur got her into her clothes and back to her spot by the fire a little after two A.M. He guessed that Chiquita knew of the movement. Spur was not worried about it. He was more concerned with getting some sleep so he could function rationally tomorrow. The deeper they penetrated Mescalero country the more the danger.

He turned on his side again and closed his eyes. Before he could drift off to sleep he heard a scuffle away from the wagon, then a man's scream of pain, and an angry eruption of Spanish that could come only from Chiquita.

Spur was on his feet, running, his .45 in his hand. Twenty steps from the wagon he saw

Chiquita kneeling, the moonlight glinting off her knife.

The blade lay against Father Clark's throat. Spur saw dark stains of fresh blood on the steel. Chiquita's brown blouse was torn open, hanging by threads, exposing her two full breasts in the moonlight.

Clark held his left arm with his right hand. Blood seeped between his fingers and there was a look of terror on the priest's face.

"He dies," Chiquita said simply.

Mother Superior Benedict hurried up. She wore a long white nightgown and took in the scene in a second. She spoke rapidly in Spanish.

Spur caught most of it. She said yes, Father Clark deserved to die for attacking her. But he was still a priest, a servant of God. Only God can punish him. God has before and he will again. Chiquita must put away the knife.

"Give me the knife, Chiquita," Spur said softly kneeling beside her.

She looked at him, her face distorted by fury, hatred and remembered pain.

"My Mescalero name in Pohati, it means knife woman who never forgets. This man is not my husband, he attacked me. He must die. It is the Mescalero way!" She moved the sharp blade until it touched the priest's throat, her eyes glinting with a fury and hatred that Spur had never seen before in any woman, Mexican, Indian or white.

TEN

Chiquita increased the pressure with the biting sharp knife against the priest's throat until a trace of blood showed.

"This man must die, it is the Mescalero way!" she said.

"It is not the Spanish way," Spur said gently. "The Mexican people are known for their fairness, for order and justice. Would your mother have said the same words you have?"

The knife pressure eased. She glanced at him, then back at the priest.

"He jumped me in the dark like a coward. Then he threw me to the ground, tore off my shirt, he touched me in my most private places. I got one hand loose and sliced his wrist. If I had not been able to do that he would have violated me. This rapist must die!"

"Your mother would not have said that, Chiquita," Spur said. "She was Mexican and proud. She suffered much for you. Wouldn't she want you to follow her way and her teachings about this situation?"

"He attacked me, like he was an animal! We Mescaleros put to death our rabid dogs. He is a rabid dog! He must die before he spreads the sickness. I will kill him."

"He will face justice, but not this way," Spur said sharply. "It can't be Mescalero justice. They abandoned you, they rejected you, they threw you out of their village and their tribe. You have no loyalty to the tribe or to its laws."

"He ripped open my shirt! He pawed me and kissed me! His hands violated me!"

Spur reached slowly toward her hand still holding the blade.

Father Clark's eyes were wide with fear, then he went limp. Unconscious, Spur figured. He put his hand over her fingers that held the blade. For a moment her hand tried to move the weapon, to slash Clark's throat. Then her arm and hand relaxed, let go of the blade and Spur caught it.

He lifted the small woman, and Mother Superior Benedict was there, her arms around the girl, talking quietly to her in Spanish and English as they walked back toward the wagon. Clark sat up at once. He had been faking.

"Suppose I should thank you, McCoy."

"I don't ask a rattlesnake for thanks when I don't kill it."

"That is some woman! Did you see the size of those . . ."

Before Clark could finish the sentence, Spur backhanded him across the mouth and he slammed backward to the ground. A line of blood came from the side of his mouth.

"I'll remember that, McCoy. One of these

nights when I'm not a priest, I'll settle with you."

"Not when you're tied up to a wagon wheel, because that's where you're going to be for the rest of the night, and every night we're on the trial."

"You wouldn't do that!"

"Watch me!"

Spur grabbed the man by his arm and towed him to the wagon. Clark held back but he did not fight, he knew he would have no chance against the larger man. To Spur, Clark was no longer a priest, he had lost any respect, rights and privileges he might have once commanded from Spur. Now Clark was simply a man, and not a good one.

Spur used rawhide, tied one end securely to Clark's wrist and forced him to sit beside the rear wagon wheel. He tied one hand at shoulder height to each side of the wheel. Clark began groaning and whining. Spur wanted to backhand him but he never hit a man tied up. Instead he threatened to dump a bucket full of dishwater on him, and Clark quieted.

When morning came, Chiquita had the cooking fire going and coffee ready. She hurried everyone, prodding them to finish their chores and get moving.

Spur sat down beside her, avoiding Teresa.

"Chiquita. Do you think we're far enough south of the Mescals so we can still travel during the daylight hours from now on?"

The half Mescalero sipped her coffee and looked at him over the rim of the cup from her deep, dark eyes. "I've been hoping so, Spur

McCoy. After today's scouting I'll tell you. We can move nearly twice as far by traveling during the day, which means we cut down our stay in Mescal territory by half. On the other hand we are twenty times as likely to be spotted by the hostiles during the day."

"If we stay over a daytime, we'll need cover, a good sized creek and lots of trees. We should be stocking firewood as we go along."

She nodded.

Spur watched her, not sure how to continue. At last he struggled with the words.

"About last night. Do you want to ride in the wagon today?"

"No. He didn't hurt me. I should have been quicker and killed him before you came. I'll do my job as usual. You don't have to worry about me. Worry about Clark."

"You don't have to be concerned about him. He's going to be tied up each night."

Chiquita looked up at Spur in a curious way that he could not read. She wore the same tight brown pants but a different shirt, this one a darker brown shade. It would blend well into the more desert like country they approached. She turned, walked to her horse and rode away. He had not seen her speak to anyone except Mother Benedict and himself.

The sisters were whispering about what had happened last night. They seemed indignant but not surprised about Clark. Some of them stared at him in open worry and anger. Spur went over and cut Clark loose from the wheel, told him to eat quickly they were about to roll.

The priest glared at Spur then rubbed his

wrists where they had been tied and did as he was told.

Two hours after they left the camp site, Chiquita rode back and signaled to Spur. He met her and they rode side by side.

"We were too quick to judge the Mescals," she said. "Less than a half hour ahead there is an old Mescalera squaw sitting in the trail. She is ancient, toothless, hairless, wasted away. She sits beside a cactus plant with three blossoms on it waiting."

"Waiting to die," Spur continued. "It is the way of the Mescaleros. Can we go around her?"

"Not without wasting a lot of time. It would cost us almost five miles."

"We'll go ahead. You talk to the missionaries. Explain about the old one."

Chiquita shook her head. "I am your scout, not their teacher. You tell them if they need to be told. I need to scout along the trail the rest of her family clan left. There were eight to ten of them, with one seven-dog dragging a travois. Don't worry, they won't see me. The old woman said she has been waiting to die for two days. The rest of the Mescals could be twenty miles to the north by now."

The scout kicked her horse and the roan gelding darted forward.

Spur took off his hat and slapped the dust out of it against his jeans pants leg. It was going to be hot again today, in the nineties somewhere. He wiped a line of sweat off his forehead, then rode over and talked with Mother Benedict. He told her there was something he needed to speak to them all about. She called in the horseback riders and brought up the three nuns from the back of the wagon. They watched Spur as he rode along beside the wagon.

"Up ahead, we're going to see an Indian. She is a Mescalero and old. You may wonder what she's doing sitting beside the trail. In many of the plains and southwest Indian tribes, life is extremely hard. Existence and enough to eat day by day are the primary goals.

"This means that every member of the tribe or family group has specific and important jobs to do. The hunters bring in game, the root gatherers dig for edible roots and tubers, the berry pickers and fruit pickers do their jobs. If one person fails to do the work, the whole tribe suffers.

"The old squaw up ahead has decided that she can no longer hold up her end of the productive life. She can't benefit the tribe any longer. She is a liability, a drain on the very existence of the other tribal members.

"So she has one final talk with her family, then sits down by the trail to die."

There were excited whispers and talk among the girls.

"Like I tell you sisters, if you don't work, you don't eat," Mother Superior Benedict said. "Only these people mean it and live by that code."

"We can help her when we get there!" Sister Mary Joseph said.

The nuns all chimed in with offers of aid. Spur held up his hand.

"No. Absolutely not. When we come up to her,

none of you is to touch her, nor try to speak to her. It would be the most kindness to the woman if you did not even look at her. She is waiting to die. It is a religious experience for these people, the last one, and they insist that it be done right."

"We just go on by?" Mother Benedict asked. "We can't even give her a sip of water?"

"No, nothing. We won't even stop the wagon."

"That's cruel, inhuman!" one of the nuns said.

"Life is cruel, unfair, and often difficult. She would be shamed in the sight of the Indian spirits if she accepted help. We will look, but not stare, we will ride past without speaking, or helping her in any way."

"How long has she been there?" Sister Teresa asked.

"Chiquita being Mescal could talk to her. The old woman said it was her second or third day. This could be her last. She had prayed all night to the spirits to take her soul today."

"How awful!" a sister said.

Someone began to cry.

Spur shook his head. "No! This is not a sad time. It is the ultimate day for this woman. Tonight she will be with the spirits. Her soul will be released of its earthly pains and ills, and she will be free."

Spur turned and rode away to the front. He saw the Indian woman beside the trail where it slanted down a gentle incline to a crossing of a deep crevase that had been cut by hundreds of years of cloudbursts hitting the desert, boiling down small ravines, then gathering here and digging a deep ditch as it all ran off quickly.

He waited a hundred yards off for the wagon, then led the mules past the woman. No one spoke. The harness jangled, the wagon creaked and groaned as it rolled past on well greased wheels. The Indian squaw did not look at them. She was covered with three or four layers of clothing and one Navajo woven rug of many colors.

One of the nuns began to cry, then a second and a third. Sister Maria turned and stared at the huddled figure, but did not speak.

A few minutes later they were past and the nuns buzzed with chatter.

Mother Superior Benedict quieted them with a glance. "If only we could be as dedicated, as unswerving, as devoted to our beliefs as she is to hers." Mother Benedict sighed, looked at the nuns. "Sisters, there will be no communicating for the next hour except in emergencies. Let us meditate on the unusual strength of the old Indian woman, and learn from it."

Chiquita met them at the noon stop. She had spotted no Mescaleros after riding up their trail of the travois for five miles. She was convinced the family unit was moving back to the more favorable country to the north, after having been perhaps as far south as Mexico.

"No other traces of Mescals?"

"None."

"Then we shall drive by day tomorrow," Spur said.

Chiquita nodded her agreement and picked at

the bones of a rabbit which had been salted down.

Father Clark had found his hidden whiskey bottle and was silently drunk in the wagon. He would eat nothing.

They rolled again. Sister Cecilia had been alternating the teams of mules. They each worked two days then had one day off. They were holding up well.

That morning they had passed through the small stream seen the day before. All of the animals had been watered well, and their water keg and barrel refilled. They gathered all of the dry dead wood they could find and tied it in bundles and bound them to the sides of the wagon box.

Now, far ahead they saw smoke. They had not seen any smoke since they left the edge of Lubbock. Chiquita went forward at once to investigate.

She came back quickly and asked Spur to ride ahead with her.

"Three small houses and the start of a cattle operation. No sense trying it way out here. Not enough grass. Not enough water. Too many Mescaleros."

"The settlers, are they hurt?" Spur asked.

"None of them hurt anymore. The Mescaleros killed everyone, took whatever they wanted and fled north. It may have been the old squaw's family. There was a travois, heavily loaded."

They rode faster then, and pulled up at the edge of the first house. Spur saw a man with his head half hacked off and his belly sliced open.

Near a well lay the body of a naked woman her legs still spread where she had been tied down and raped.

Spur loosened his .45 in the leather.

"Let's go in and see if anyone is still alive."

ELEVEN

Spur swung down from his bay and stared at the two bodies. He knew there would be more. Three small ranchers had evidently tried to defy the odds and started ranching far out from anyone else. Land was probably not theirs, squatters. Evidently they had settled too far into the Mescaleros traditional lands.

His six-gun was out as he ran to the first house and looked inside. A six year old boy sprawled on his stomach on the living room floor. A large pool of blood had seeped from where his face once had been. A woman lay beside a kitchen table in the next room, her clothes gone, her crotch bloody, one breast cut off.

It went on and on. Spur holstered his weapon. There was no one to fear here anymore. The pain, the torture, the rape, the killing was over.

In the third house in the small compound he found only two bodies. So far he had counted four men and six women. Multiple marriages?

Ten children had been cut down before they had a chance to live.

He kicked a wall in the last house and leaned against it a moment. So much death.

The sound went past him at first. Just another small remembered noise in a place where there had been joy and laughter only two days before. The small sound came again, and he caught it, turned and went to the next room.

A house cat?

Now it was a cry. A baby's cry!

He rushed through the rooms, searching in every place where a baby could be hidden. He had heard the cry first in the small kitchen. There was nowhere to hide a baby, not in there. Maybe. He began pulling out drawers. One was a sugar bin, the next for home milled flour . . .

Two soft blue eyes stared up at him. The face twisted into a scowl and quickly cried.

Spur picked the blanket covered baby from the flour and brushed it off. He met Chiquita in the yard, the baby crying now with anger and hunger.

Chiquita let a small smile cross her face, then she took the baby, lay it on an outside table and unwrapped it. She cleaned the small white female body, found some towels and tore them into diapers for the infant, then wrapped her in a clean, dry blanket.

The well had not been polluted, so Spur drew water and they let the baby, perhaps a month old, sip at the water and suck it from their fingers.

Soon the small girl quieted and slept.

"I should bury them," Spur said looking at the bodies in the yard.

"A strange and pagan custom," Chiquita said. "Why put their bodies under the ground where their spirits will be trapped forever? They are better this way."

"Twenty-three are dead," Spur said. He had satisfied his curiosity about the men-women ratio. He had found a Book of Mormon in one of the houses.

"They were Latter Day Saints," Spur said. "I have no idea what they were doing way out here."

Spur held the child while Chiquita walked around the houses again and the three corrals. She came back after fifteen minutes of examining the grounds.

"Ten to twelve Mescalero braves on foot," she said. "They drove away nearly thirty head of beef and four horses." She hesitated. "They also took with them five white women, three full grown and two younger ones."

Spur slammed his fist into the table.

"They left here a little over a day ago. That's why the child is still alive."

"Let's get back to the wagon," Spur said. "We'll make a detour around this place."

"I agree. We slant more to the south. The family group that raided these houses has enough cattle to last them for years, if they would settle down in a valley somewhere. But they won't. They will kill too many beef too quickly. Some of the steers will wander off and die in the desert. Some will be stolen by other

Mescals. Natural hunters and raiders like the Mescals make rotten cowboys.''

They rode back to the wagon which was still half a mile away. Spur carried the small bundle.

Traces of smoke could still be seen from the buildings as Chiquita angled the wagon more to the south. Two of the nuns had ridden to meet Spur and when they saw the baby, they squealed in delight.

The wagon stopped as the nuns gathered round the small one. They sobered as Spur told them she was the only survivor at the houses.

Mother Superior looked at her nuns.

"Sister Mary Joseph, you had three younger sisters at home. You will be responsible for our small visitor. We have no milk, no baby bottle. You will take over the place where I had been sleeping for the nursery. We'll talk about feeding her. What should we call her?''

A dozen names echoed around the wagon.

"Blossom,'' Chiquita said. "She is a small flowering blossom on this barren land. The last blossom of a whole settlement.''

It was decided.

Sister Joseph took the bundle, moved into the front of the wagon and began preparing food for the small one, now named Blossom. The food all had to be liquid. She soaked dried fruits, made thin gravies with flour, made sugar water and fashioned a sugar tit on a small jar and a piece of white cloth the liquid could seep through.

It would work.

Chiquita rode up beside Spur and stared at him until he glanced at her.

"It is the time of the Great Battle?" Spur asked.

"You've heard of that?"

"Most people who try to live in this area know about it, fear it."

She waved one hand as if wiping out a sand painting. "No, I've heard nothing about the Great Battle around here. There has been little talk lately of driving the Mexicans and the Americans out of the historic Apache lands. The old men talk little of it. Some of the younger braves have never heard the story. Most realize there are too many roundeyes now, it is impossible."

"Then all this sudden raiding? Why does the army think the Mescaleros are getting ready to go on the warpath?"

"Ask the army. All roundeyes forget the Apache and especially the Mescaleros are raiders by nature. We make war for sport, we Mescals live by raiding, not by hunting or digging in the ground or growing strange animals."

"Like the steer."

"And the horse and the pig, yes."

"And those twenty-three souls back there lying dead in the hot sun?"

"A chance, a surprise target, an easy kill not to be passed by."

"A chance at life, or a chance at death. At least one of them has the possibility of living through it," Spur said.

"Blossom will live, she is a strong baby or she would have died already. She will live."

"Let's talk about moving ahead. We're now well south of most of the Mescalero areas. What's your suggestion about traveling during the day?"

"Yes, move in the light."

"I agree. We'll start pushing harder, daylight to dusk, try for twenty miles a day. Today included."

Chiquita looked up with a new appreciation showing in her eyes. Quickly she hid it, turned. "I'll check ahead for the best spot to stop." She glanced up at the burning sun. "We have five more hours before dusk." She touched the roan gelding's flanks with her boot heels and galloped away toward the southwest.

Spur told the missionaries about the new plans. He also said that he and Chiquita had decided that the raiders on the ranches were part of the same family group of Mescaleros who had left the old squaw to die.

"So we'll push farther and faster during the day," Spur told the sisters. "If we can move twenty miles a day instead of fifteen, we can be in Roswell three or four days quicker. But more important, we can cross the danger zone here that much faster."

The nuns were holding up better than he had expected. Most of them were used to hard work, and the riding and camp work was like a vacation to them. Their sunbonnets were showing signs of wear, and they tried to wash their spare pants and shirts whenever they came to a stream.

Spur left his bay and walked around the wagon. The spare mule team plodded along behind the Conestoga. The wheels were getting a little dry on axle grease. He would take care of that chore tonight. Spur spent five minutes walking beside the mules, checking the harness, the doubletrees and the traces and driving lines. He found no problems.

He tied the bay on a lead line beside the mules and jumped up to the driver's bench in front.

"Spell you a while with the reins, driver?"

Mother Benedict smiled:

"Yes, and I can play with Blossom. She's such a cute little baby!"

"First, we need to talk."

She looked up quickly. "About Father Clark."

"Yes. Back in Lubbock there was the spectacle of the whore house, and then assault and battery and jail. Now we have attempted rape. Another thirty seconds and Chiquita would have killed him."

"Yes, I know that, Mr. McCoy. So did Father Clark. I don't expect any more trouble from him."

"When we get to Roswell, I think we should turn him over to the sheriff with charges."

"Oh, my, we could never do that. The church takes care of its own whenever possible. That's partly why the bishop sent Father Clark out here."

"Do we have to wait until he kills a girl?"

"By all the saints in heaven, Mr. McCoy, I pray that we don't have that happen. He used to be such a fine priest, such an outstanding pastor."

"Mother Benedict. Priest or no priest, if he tries anything like this again, I'll turn him in an and swear out the complaint as soon as we get to Roswell. You might tell him this if it happens to be convenient, even if it isn't convenient."

"That I will, Mr. McCoy. Now let me play with our small one."

Spur turned the two teams a little more to the west to bypass some breaks showing ahead in the plains. It could mean some relief from the high plateau of a low range of hills or perhaps a large river.

Three hours later, Chiquita returned, and Spur turned the driving over to Sister Cecilia who had a delicate touch with the eight pieces of leather in her hands.

Chiquita waited for him to mount and ride to her.

"Three more miles ahead," she said. "It's a good sized sink and plenty of water for the animals. Maybe even time for a quick bath."

"Bad for the skin," Spur said.

She grinned. "You're teasing. Sometimes it's hard to tell." She pointed. "Just to the left of those breaks. It's about twenty feet below the rest of the prairie and makes a perfect windbreak."

"Any sign?"

"None. We may be lucky. I'll ride ahead and get a fire started."

"You can have a bath, too," Spur said.

She whipped the horse away from him, turned and smiled over her shoulder, then was gone.

Father Clark came out of his sanctuary. He was almost sober. He took one of the horses and rode. Spur watched him for a while, but he was simply plodding along with the wagon, his head down as if in thought, sitting the saddle well. He must have some reason for riding the horse, but Spur could not figure it out. Unless he wanted to establish a riding pattern late in the afternoon. Then when they were within a few miles of Roswell he could ride, slip away and head for town without them and make his escape from the law.

With a man like Wilbur Clark, anything was possible, Spur thought.

An hour later the mules stopped and danced a strange jig. Spur had been a hundred yards ahead, and now he came charging back on his bay mare to see what the problem was.

The rifle shot caught him by surprise. He listened to it echoing in the distance and hoped there was not a Mescalero within ten miles of them.

He saw Mother Benedict stand up on the front of the wagon, the rifle in her hands.

Even before he arrived he saw what had been the problem. A rattlesnake lay between the mules. It had been surprised and the sharp hooves had sliced off six inches of its tail and its rattlers. The rattles popped and crackled as the muscles in the severed section made the dismembered part dance as they spasmed.

The snake had tried to coil and strike, but the natural instinct of coiling was wrong somehow, and the strikes at the mule's dancing legs had been short and inaccurate.

The dead snake lay between the lead team, its head blown half off by the big .52 caliber Spencer round.

Spur moved the teams and kicked the dead

snake away to the side and the mules settled down. He looked at the seat in front of the canvas.

"Glad you're on our side. Not a lot of rattlers out here yet. Wonder where that one came from?"

"Sunning himself. By the time I saw him the lead team was stomping all over the creature."

Spur waved them forward.

An hour later they eased down an incline into the hollow and found the water and gush of green trees in the two acre oasis.

Camping, cooking and the other routines of the end of the day were second nature to them by now. Each of the nuns did her job with surprising skill and good humor. Spur admitted he had never been on such a pleasant wagon trip. If it wasn't for Clark it would be ideal.

Sister Ruth set up her small reflector oven and baked biscuits for them, made bacon gravy without the aid of milk and added fried potatoes and onions for night's meal. They refilled the water kegs and as dusk settled down four of the sisters went to the left and took quick baths in the surprisingly cool water.

Spur, Clark and Mother Benedict sat around the fire until the nuns came back chattering and cool after their bath. As soon as it became dark, Spur began walking his guard duty, then settled down near the mules and horses and listened to the new night sounds.

Several species of birds used the oasis as a sanctuary, and they talked to each other at night. He heard the hooting of a big owl somewhere far below them, and the wail of a solitary coyote. Then nothing.

The Big Dipper wheeled around the North Star. Night feeding rabbits scampered nearby.

He started to stand to make another circuit.

"Don't move," Chiquita said six feet from him. He knew her voice at once.

She slid to the ground beside him.

"McCoy, I think it's time we had a long, quiet talk." She picked up his hand it put it over her breasts. She put one hand behind his neck and pulled his head down to hers and kissed him hard on the lips.

When it ended she pressed against him. "Spur McCoy, I've seen you watching me, and I've been watching you. I want you, right now. I want you to take off my clothes and show me that you're as good a lover as I think you are."

TWELVE

Spur's hand slowly kneaded her breast through the shirt. He leaned back so he could see her clearly in the moonlight.

"What was all that knife work, that 'touch me and I slice your face off' business?"

She smiled. "For some reason men think I'm easy to get in bed. Maybe it's my big titties. So I am fierce, hard, and they stay away." She smiled again and kissed him. When she pulled back she continued. "They stay away until I invite them to come play. Is that not a good idea?"

She unbuttoned her blouse. "All of the nuns are sleeping, including your little friend Teresa. I will show you I am better at making love than she is."

"You noticed."

"Of course, I was on guard." She let the blouse fall away from her shoulders and turned her breasts to him. They were fuller than he had thought, heavy, with pink aerolas and large pink nipples. He bent and kissed one, then the other one.

She shivered for a few moments, then watched him. "Yes, gringo, bite me and chew on them."

Her hands worked down his chest unbuttoning his shirt, then loosening his belt and working on the fasteners of his fly. Spur felt the heat surging from her breasts. It was as if they were on fire and he had to put them out with his mouth. He licked them and nibbled on the pink morsels, then sucked one deeply into his mouth.

Chiquita gasped, suddenly, her face clouded, then she relaxed and smiled. She pulled away and stood.

"Come down this way," she whispered. "Sometimes I make noise when I am loving."

They walked fifty yards to the far end of the sink, and settled down on soft green grass. Slowly she stripped off his boots and pants, then his underwear.

"Oh, my, yes, gringo, I like your big friend." She nestled at his crotch, kissing his erection, then pulling it into her mouth and pumping back and forth until he touched her head and she came away and kissed him.

"You liked my mouth on you?" she asked.

"Yes." He ran his hands down her sleek sides to her pants, then brushed fingers across her belly to her crotch and rubbed at her through the cloth. He touched the buttons but she held his hand.

She pushed him to his back and moved lower until her breasts were at his phallus. She held her breasts together around him and looked up.

"Tit fuck me," she said.

Spur grinned and slowly began thrusting his big member, stabbing upward and sliding past her two big breasts which Chiquita held together around him. After a dozen strokes she giggled like a school girl and rolled away from him.

She caught his hand and moved it to her fly. Slowly he undid the buttons, and edged the trousers down. She helped him. Under the pants she wore a pure silk undergarment. He had never seen anything like it. It was much shorter than the usual drawers of cotton that most women wore. It gathered at her waist and came down halfway on each leg, but was soft, silky and so smooth.

He pushed his hand under the top and downward past the soft cloth along satiny flank and belly to a nest of dark fur.

Chiquita shivered and whimpered. He looked at her. She lay rigid on the grass, staring straight upward at the sky. He stopped his hand, bent and kissed her lips gently. He pulled back his hand and kissed her again, then put his arms around her and held her gently.

"Chiquita, little flower. You have never made love with a man, have you?"

"Of course, many times." She said it sharply, but there was no foundation of truth in her tone.

He kissed her again. "Did a man take you by force once, several years ago and it hurt terribly?"

Slowly she nodded.

"And ever since you've been wanting and

wondering and hoping it would be good when it could be done in love, but you were also much afraid?''

Again she nodded. She turned her face toward him and cried softly. When the tears were gone, she wiped her eyes and watched his face.

"You won't laugh at me?"

"Never."

"I was about sixteen, and in Lubbock, just after I had left the nuns. This man was drunk and grabbed me off the sidewalk and pushed me into a dark alley. He held one hand over my mouth and tore off my clothes. He was rough and it hurt for two weeks. That's why I cut men who come near me. I learned well."

He kissed her eyes, and then her nose, and at last her lips.

"Chiquita, making love with someone should be soft and gentle, with each person trying to make the other pleased and happy and satisfied. It's easiest to make love with a person you really love." He leaned back and held her close, her small body tightly against his. She was shivering again.

"I think we better get our clothes back on."

"No! I'm so close. And I . . . I like you, Spur McCoy. Isn't like enough? I mean . . . I want to know what it's like to do it and not hurt and not be angry and scared. I want you to help me make love the right way, Spur McCoy!"

"Damn!"

"Did I say something wrong?"

"Why now, Chiquita?"

"You saw what happened back at those ranches. We . . .we could be in the same kind of situation, at any time. I . . . I want to know how good making love can be. Is it like I have heard? I don't want to remember only the pain, the anger, and the shame."

"It would be so much better in Roswell, safely snuggled in a big bed with the lights on and some fine wine and cheese . . ."

"Now, please, Spur."

He kissed her softly, then harder and the flames in him rose up and he wanted to show her how gentle a man could be. He touched the silk undergarment again and her hand helped him. Slowly they pulled off the shimmering silk and put it to one side.

She shivered and he kissed her lips, then both her breasts, then his hand touched the soft fur and she gasped.

"Chiquita, making love is the most beautiful thing two people can ever do together. It is magic, it is wonder, it is the joining together of two people in a feast of desire, and respect and love and beauty. Making love develops the most powerful feelings that most people ever have."

As he talked quietly his hand stroked the fur, working lower and lower. His fingers probed gently through the black hairs and brushed against the soft, moist labia.

"Oh! Oh, Spur! Touch me there again!"

He did. She murmured deep in her throat, reached and pressed his hand again to her outer lips. She began nibbling at his ear.

Softly he moved his fingers, stroking the moist lips, then lifting higher and finding the magic node and strummed it twice.

She frowned, then looked at him.

He hit it five, six, seven times and Chiquita gasped and then shivered and moaned in the start of a climax that shook her like a willow in a tornado. She trembled and jolted as the vibrations coursed through her. She found his mouth and kissed him as the tremors faded and passed.

For a moment she didn't move, then she grabbed his face with both hands.

"That was marvelous! Nothing like that happened to me last time. Why?"

He kissed her cheek and smiled. "Because you were terrified, you were being assaulted, raped. Now you are relaxed, receptive, wanting to understand."

She nodded, serious. Then grinned. "Now show me the rest."

His hand caressed her labia, then he probed with a finger and she gasped. Spur eased her knees apart and knelt between them. He entered her slowly, gently and she was ready and wanting him.

When they were locked together she smiled. "This is almost as good as the other."

Spur could not hold back any longer and he jolted suddenly, erupting into her and she pounded back against him in a natural movement that surprised and pleased her. As he finished his climax she soared into a second one of her own, and again trembled and moaned as the spasms lanced through her again and again.

They both gasped trying to get enough air into their lungs. They lay side by side, staring at the stars. Impulsively she leaned over and kissed him.

"Thank you, Spur McCoy. Tomorrow night

we'll have to wait until later for my second lesson." She sat up and scrambled into her clothes. He dressed as she did and when they both were fully clothed again, she leaned over and kissed his cheek.

"You were right, I did have a bath this afternoon." She laughed softly and they walked back toward the wagons. The Big Dipper's open cup was almost due west of the North Star. By four A.M. it would be directly below the North Star so the star could fall into the cup if it came loose in the sky.

She looked up at the Big Dipper. "Your watch is almost over. Are you going to be brave and take the rest of the night?"

"Might as well, I couldn't sleep much now, anyway," he said.

She touched her lips to his cheek. "Not a chance. I do my share, and it's my watch until dawn." She hestitated. "But I guarantee you one thing. The next time I break into your hotel room, I'll use your bed for something better than just sitting on." She grinned, and ran to put her blankets near the wagon, then began circling the small camp.

Spur walked to the wagon, picked up his blankets and found a stretch of grass away from the horses. He had checked and Clark was tied securely inside the wagon. It might be an unneeded precaution, but the madman would be tied up every night until he was safely inside a jail cell.

McCoy thought about Chiquita for a moment, smiled at the memory of the past hour and faded into sleep.

The cry of a baby woke Spur a half hour before dawn. Most of the camp was up and moving around. Three of the nuns were trying to feed the baby. Sister Joseph came and provided the right cloth tipped bottle of sugar water and Blossom settled down for a quick meal and another nap.

The rest of the travelers came awake and another day on the trail began. Spur had only coffee and a biscuit and some jam for breakfast. He applied more axle grease to the hubs of the four wheels, and knew he could soon have to take one wheel off to completely regrease it. But for now it could wait.

They were rolling by the time Mother Benedict's pocket watch said five-thirty. They were determined to get in a good twenty miles that day.

Father Clark moved from his bed to the front seat on the wagon and took over the driving chores. Mother Superior watched him for an hour, then decided she could trust the job to him and went into the wagon with the baby. It had been years since she had a baby so young all to herself. If they kept Blossom she would be spoiled absolutely rotten.

Spur rode ahead to check the trail and found Chiquita waiting for him a half mile across the high plateau. He had lost track of the days, but guessed they were in New Mexico now. There might be a survey marker somewhere, but most boundaries in the west were indistinct and not that important with land valued at five cents an acre.

Chiquita rode over by the side and leaned in to

be kissed. He touched her lips and she clung for a moment, then sat down in her saddle.

"No sign that has anything to do with Mescaleros."

They rode half a mile without speaking, then Spur touched her shoulder.

"How was your mother captured?"

Chiquita watched him a moment, then her face softened, and she pretended to throw cornmeal to the four points of the compass.

"Did you know that in some Indian tribes, when a person dies, the name is never mentioned again? The idea is that the person's soul can not be in two places at once, and the constant repetition of the name keeps the spirit bound to the earth.

"I think we're safe now, my mother has been dead for nearly five years. We lived far to the south in Texas near the border, and the Mescaleros living in Mexico often swarmed across raiding the smaller villages. The Indians waited until the men went to the fields to work the land, then they swept in and took any horses and cattle they could find, and now and then caught a young woman to take back as a special prize.

"Mother was in the last house in the village toward the border and as they drove a dozen horses past they charged through the house, found her, bound her hands and feet and threw her over a horse and carried her away.

"She was the property of the brave who caught her, and he married her as his second squaw. Only a few weeks later this branch of the Mescaleros picked up and moved four hundred miles north into central New Mexico, to the more traditional lands of the Mescals. They settled in the mountains and for a few years time stood still for them and life was as it had been fifty years before. They hunted, they raided other tribes, and now and then they attacked a roundeye who wandered too close to their lodges.

"I was born exactly a year after Mother's capture, given an Indian name, and grew up learning both Spanish and the strange mixture of Spanish and the Apache dialect. When I was five, Mother and I tried to run away, but they caught us. Mother had her nose pierced by a hot nail as punishment. She kept the scar for as long as she lived.

"Then a year later she made so much trouble for my father, that he left us beside the trail one day with the clear understanding that we should not come back to his tipi. Mother carried me and we both walked and at last came to a ranch house where they took us in. Eventually we got back to Mother's village. But they threw us out of there, too."

"Because she had been captured by the Indians?"

"Yes, and because of me. Obviously Mother had *relations* with the savages. So we wandered. A few years later mother died and I was on my own, really on my own. I begged on the streets for a while. I existed. The nuns found me. Here I am."

"You mentioned a brother once."

"Yes, I never knew much about him. He's a Breed as well, but he stayed with the tribe. He's out there somewhere." She frowned. "Every Mescal I see I'll be thinking that he could be my brother."

"He will kill you if he gets the chance," Spur said. "You can't let the thought of him interfere. . . ."

"I know!" She looked at him and there were tears sliding down her pretty face. "I know, but I can do it. I will forget that I might have a brother out there somewhere. My brother the Mescalero Apache! If he attacks us, I will kill him without a moment's hesitation."

Chiquita looked at him from tear filled eyes.

"I must," she said, "I must!"

THIRTEEN

Spur kissed away a tear as it ran down Chiquita's cheek and hugged her around her shoulders as they both sat on their horses.

"Just forget about maybe having a brother out there," Spur told her. "There is a thousand to one chance that he's not even in this part of the country. For the next two weeks, you've got to forget all about even having a brother."

He lifted her chin with his hand so she looked into his eyes.

"Agreed?" Spur asked.

"Yes, agreed." She wiped at her eyes, then moved away from him a few feet. "I'm all right. Don't fret about me." She took a deep breath and shivered, then straightened her shoulders. "About last night. . . I don't know how to talk about it. I don't know the right words . . . Just wonderful!" Her eyes were bright now with memories, and her smile came back, warm and honest and open. A man could do a lot worse picking a woman.

"I know what you felt, Chiquita. I felt it too. Yes, wonderful says it."

"Good." She looked to the west, the rolling high plateau meandered forward. "There's a small little bluff of some kind out there about five or six miles. I'm going to get on it and find out what I can see to the west and north. Something still bothers me about the Mescals. They must be here somewhere. If I'm missing them, and they know we're here, coming through . . ." She left it unfinished. They both knew what would happen. "I'll be back for lunch." She smiled. "Does making love always leave you so hungry? I'm so starved that I could eat a cactus blossom!"

Spur laughed and watched her respond, then she waved and rode off to the west. Spur pulled his reddish brown mare around and headed back to the wagon.

For the next two days they rolled along over the dirt and sand and dry washes and slight rise and falls of the prairie.

They found no signs of Mescaleros, they saw no game, they found no new water. The small drum was empty, the larger barrel was getting low. Everyone was warned to go easy on water. At places there were miles and miles of only the scantiest of vegetation, a few grasses, some small sagebrush bushes, but no trees, no streams and no brush.

The seventh day of the trip, Spur and Chiquita held a conference, and decided to swing back north toward a water hole she knew of. It should still contain water this early in the year, and they could get there before it ran out. If Indians were there they would have to risk it.

Father Clark had been a model of priestly behavior during the last two days. He was polite, sober, even held morning mass one day. He drove the wagon half the time now, but Spur still tied him securely at night. He submitted with little complaint.

But he was planning, Wilbur Clark never had been a man to let someone get the best of him. Now as he drove the wagon he watched the nuns. He enjoyed seeing them in the pants and shirts. Two of the shirts were too small for the women and outlined their breasts dramatically.

He remembered an early parish he had in Louisiana where he had dug a peephole through the wall of the nuns' bathroom. Glorious! He had seen more naked female bodies that six months than before or since. He picked out the one with the least inhibitions, and worked on her slowly, and a month later went to bed with her. It had been with her permission. She loved to be loved. After that they made love every three nights for almost three months. Then she became pregnant and she ran away before it showed.

He had hastily asked to be moved to another parish where the girl could not find him.

Yes! Women! His vow of chastity had long been an empty shell. He needed a woman again, it had been too long. Two nuns rode by on the horses, and he decided. Sister Mary Francis. She had a cute little ass in those pants, and she definitely had the biggest tits of any of the nuns.

She would be the one.

He guessed that she was twenty-two or three. Had a face he could stand, but oh, her body! His hand wrapped the reins around the brake handle for a minute and he pushed his right hand into his pocket. The bottom had been ripped loose and he wormed his hand to his crotch. Just watching the nuns gave him a boner. He squirmed to let it straighten out and then sighed. He would work on her for two or three days. No, there was no secret place, no spot where they could be alone.

It would have to be a one time conquest, perhaps when she was alone getting water, or gathering wood. Yes, tonight when they stopped, after supper, but before he was tied up. Yes, that would be the timing. If only they could find some woods.

He kept his hand in his pocket massaging slowly as he thought back over his conquests. At first he had been surprised how easy it had been. When he was only two years out of seminary and serving in a large church as a fourth pastor, he had caught two nuns in a lesbian tryst.

He had lectured both of them for fifteen minutes, requiring them to remain unclothed while he reminded them of their vows, and the unnaturalness of their behavior. Then he told the older one to dress and to leave. He told her he would keep her secret if she were extremely pious and hardworking. She agreed, dressed and left.

The younger nun was much prettier, and slender with good breasts. He sat beside her and told her what she had done was wrong, that it was much more interesting if a man did the same things. She was trapped, knowing she could not deny him for fear of being exposed to the Mother Superior.

He had made love three times to the woman that afternoon, and the next week he arranged that three of them could be alone in a locked room and he had been royally entertained.

He had learned quickly that there was always a chance for female companionship close at hand. If not in church circles, then certainly in the bawdy houses and fancy women rooms of the town. Whores seemed to delight in servicing a priest!

That night just after the supper stop, Sister Mary Francis wandered along a dry streambed hunting branches or drift wood she could claim for the fire. It was a half hour to dusk.

Father Clark slid away from the wagon, angled the other way behind a slight rise and ran hard around it to come up behind Sister Francis. She had bent over to pick up some wood and Father Clark growled in his throat the way the pants outlined her buttocks. He slid up quietly, then put one hand around her from behind covering her mouth. His other hand grabbed one of her breasts.

"Sister Francis, don't be afraid," he said gently. She tried to turn to look at him. "You know me, Sister, Father Clark. I won't hurt you. No matter what you've heard, I've never made love to a woman who didn't agree."

His hand began to fondle and rub her breast. His erection jolted up full and hard and he pressed it against her side. Her eyes were wild, still frightened.

"Francis, have you ever made love? Ever slept with a man and had his big cock pushed up inside your soft, wet pussy?"

Her eyes flared and Sister Francis shook her head.

"Really? I'm surprised. Such a pretty girl. Would you like to right now, quickly before anyone misses us?"

Her eyes clouded and again she shook her head.

"It would be a thrilling experience," he said. Father Clark unbuttoned her shirt front with one hand, keeping the other over her mouth. His hand went inside her shirt and under the thin chemise onto her bare breasts.

"Oh, tits!" he said gently. "Wonderful, marvelous tits!" He spread her shirt and lifted the chemise so he could see them. Not as large as he had thought, but a good double handful. He squeezed them, and played with the nipples until they hardened.

"Francis, just you and me. Nobody else will ever know." She stared the other way. He tried to press her to the ground but she was stronger than he figured. His free hand went between her legs and rubbed until she pulled her legs together.

"Come on, Francis. It will be wonderful, it will be so good you'll want to do it every night." His hand ripped off her blouse and then the chemise so she stood naked to the waist. His head bent to her breasts where he licked and then chewed on one delicious mound.

146

Sister Francis had been moving her face under his hand, until at last she had it in the right spot. She opened her mouth and bit one of his fingers. Blood spurted, Father Clark howled in pain and anger. He jerked his hand from her mouth and Mary Francis screamed so loud the Mescaleros in Mexico could have heard her.

Clark pulled back his hand and slapped her. She reeled away a step and he doubled up his fist and punched her in the face with a roundhouse right he had used in the army. Mary Francis jolted to one side, lost her balance and fell, her head striking a foot high boulder jutting from the sand of the dry stream bed.

She rolled to one side and lay still.

Spur McCoy had run fastest. He slammed a .45 slug between Clark's legs.

"Don't move even an inch, or I'll blow your brains out!" Spur called from fifty feet up the hill. Clark hesitated as if to decide what to do, then slowly he raised his hands.

"She fell down. She was airing out her shirt, I guess when I came back from my walk . . ."

Spur interrupted the words with another .45 shot, aiming precisely and thundering the big slug into Clark's upper left arm. The force of the blow knocked him down and blasted him two yards to the rear.

The other nuns had run up. Mother Superior took one look at the scene and hurried to Sister Francis. She cradled her head in her lap, pulling the tan shirt over the unconscious nun's breasts.

Spur kept his weapon trained on Clark where he whined in the dirt.

"Bad?" he asked. "I got here just as he

punched her and her head hit that rock."

Mother Superior Benedict stared hotly at Father Clark for a moment. "Yes, Mr. McCoy, it is bad. Her head must have hit the rock extremely hard. She's unconscious, her breathing is light and ragged. Help me get her shirt on."

Spur held the white shoulders as Mother Benedict worked Francis's arms into the sleeves, then buttoned her shirt.

McCoy picked her up and they went back toward the wagon. He turned to Clark.

"You can stay right there and rot as far as I'm concerned," Spur said. "After this, you have no excuse to go on living."

Mother Superior motioned to one of the nuns who went to the priest and bound up his still bleeding arm.

"Our Lord Jesus judges and God punishes, Mr. McCoy. They are not our responsibilities, or rights."

"Begging your pardon, Mother Benedict. But with scum like that one, I do quite a bit of judging and punishing."

"He's still a priest in God's service."

They lay Sister Francis on the soft blankets spread in the back of the wagon. Mother Benedict sat beside her, cradling her head on her lap. Tears touched the older eyes and wetness dripped onto the young woman below.

Spur touched Sister Francis's throat for a pulse. It came weakly, and not regular. Her breathing was also shallow. He scowled and stepped back from the wagon.

Clark and the two nuns had walked to the

camp. The nuns rushed to the end of the wagon to ask about Sister M. Francis.

Spur found a half-inch rope and tied a hangman's noose. He fitted it around Clark's neck and cinched it up.

"Clark, if I had a handy tree you would be a dead man in about fifteen minutes."

"Shoot me, it's quicker."

"Not a chance. I'd want to watch you struggle and kick, see your eyes bulge out and your breath come in smaller and smaller gasps. I wouldn't let the noose break your neck, that's too fast. It would strangle you slowly, making you suffer for as long as possible."

"You wouldn't do that to a human being," Clark said.

"No, but for you the term does not apply. In the morning I'll find an ant hill. We'll leave you spread eagled over the side of the hill. That way you'll be of some value. The ants will eat on your corpse for six months or more. Them and the buzzards."

Spur used the loose end of the rope and tied Clark's hands behind him.

"You can't kill me, there are witnesses. You'd hang for it yourself."

Spur spun around, his hand flared out and slapped Clark across the face, making him stumble three steps away.

"Don't ever say *can't* to me again, you shitface! I'm a United States lawman, I give ORDERS to the U.S. Marshalls. I can gun you down, write out a one paragraph report and that will be the last of it. What's more important, it would be the last of you!"

Spur pointed to the wagon wheel. Clark sat down in front of it and Spur tied him securely to the spokes, leaving his arms behind him.

McCoy went to the back of the wagon. Mother Superior had been crying again.

"How can something like this happen, Mr. McCoy? This poor girl was minding her own business, doing more than she had to to help with the trip, and now . . . now . . ."

Spur touched the limp wrist, then moved his hand to her throat and felt for a pulse. The beat was so weak that it was almost not there.

"I know her parents. I promised to take care of her. Her mother told her not to come way out here in the wilderness. But Mary Francis wanted to come. She said she was needed. She had prepared to teach, now was her chance."

The other sisters were putting cold cloths on her forehead. The ugly wound was just over her ear. Blood had oozed and ran down her neck. They kept it wiped up and a compress covered the wound now.

Someone lit a lantern and hung it on the high hook down from the heavy wooden box.

"Mr. McCoy! What can we do? I don't know what might help!" Mother Benedict let tears seep out of her eyes as she held the girl in her lap.

"Keep her head up, use the cold cloths," Spur said. "That's all I can suggest. Not even a trained physician could do much more. It is out of our hands."

Spur looked out of the wagon at Clark. He was still in place.

Mother Benedict gave a startled little cry. She

caught the young face and watched it, felt for a pulse.

Spur was beside her in a rush. He could find no pulse. He pinched her nostrils closed for several seconds, but there was no reaction. McCoy reached over and slowly closed the lifeless eyelids to cover the staring eyes.

"She's gone, Mother Benedict."

Spur McCoy turned and marched to the front wheel and stared down at the killer who sat there.

"I'm going to kill you, Clark. I don't know how yet, but I'll decide by morning. I'm going to execute you for the murder of Sister Mary Francis!"

FOURTEEN

Spur's hand hovered over his holstered .45 for several seconds, his fingers twitching, his whole body rigid with fury, as he stared at Father Clark. Then he gritted his teeth and turned slowly. He took two strides to the side of the wagon and pulled off the spade fastened there. For a moment he hefted it, wondering if he could cut off Clark's head with one strong thrust of the spade at the man's neck if it were held to the ground.

He might find out tomorrow.

Mother Superior Benedict slid down from the back of the wagon and hurried up to Spur.

"Mr. McCoy. We simply must not take any harsh action against Father Clark. He is still a priest, a vessel of God, a holy man. We have no authority over him. I know you feel strongly about Sister Francis's death. In a way it was an accident. He had no intention of harming her."

"Just raping her." Spur stared at the nun, his eyes still glowing with his anger. "According to the law a death occurring in the commission of a

153

felony is murder. He's guilty." Spur rubbed his mouth with the back of his hand. "I just want to see justice done, Mother. One way or another that man is going to pay with his life. That's a promise."

Spur turned and carried the shovel out of the low dry stream bed. Six feet above the narrow water course he found a level place. It would take a tremendous amount of water to touch it here. He began to dig.

For an hour he struggled in the half light of the moon. He threw dirt, squared up the hole, digging deeper. Spur pulled off his shirt and his browned torso glistened with sweat in the coolness of the night air.

He went down four feet for the narrow grave, then jumped out and looked at it.

One life gone.

One life ended so quickly, so uselessly.

One killer still breathing.

It was not right.

Mother Benedict walked up and watched him a moment. Her fingers were working on her rosary. He saw her lips moving in the moonlight.

"Mr. McCoy, I know you wouldn't approve so we did it already. We carried Sister Francis to where Father Clark was tied so he could give her the last rites. This was extremely important. We put her habit on her, so she can be buried in it."

"With first light, Mother Benedict. Just so Clark has nothing to do with it."

She bobbed her head, as if she had assumed that.

"Thank you, Spur McCoy, for digging the

grave. It would have been hard for us. You're a good man."

She left, walking the thirty yards back to the wagon. Spur slammed the spade down into the mound of dirt wishing Clark had been under it.

Clark had to die. Seldom had Spur seen a man who deserved it more than this one. The fact that he was a priest carried no weight with McCoy whatsoever. He killed, he must die. Simple justice.

Chiquita had hovered in the background after the attempted rape and the injury and then death played out. The violence was all too familiar to her. She had rebelled against it before, and she would again. Now she came to Spur and touched his arm.

He whirled, surprised.

"It's me!" she said quickly knowing he could not tell at once who it was in the partial moonlight.

"Yes. It is quiet out there?"

"So far. We have been lucky, threading a needle between the Mescalero hunters and a few travelers."

"We need another week of luck."

"You may be asking for too much." She pointed to Clark. "What happens to him?"

"If I had a tree tall enough, I'd hang him."

"You're a vigilante?"

"No, a lawman, a U.S. lawman with jurisdiction. He could always die while trying to escape."

Chiquita smiled but Spur saw only the hardness. "Or the Mescaleros could sneak into camp at night and kill only Clark," she said softly.

"No, that job is mine, one way or the other, his hide is all mine."

The next morning they buried Sister Mary Francis. Mother Superior read a simple ceremony. Spur carried her into the grave, lay her out with her hands folded on her chest and holding wild flowers. He leaped out of the hole and stood by, as uncomfortable as he always was at funerals. When the service was over, he sent the women away, and slowly shoved the dirt and rocks back into the grave. He did not look at Sister Francis's starkly white face as the earth slowly covered it.

Spur put a cross on the top of the rocks he had piled over the grave. No animals could get to it, and only a cloudburst would let water reach it. The cross was made of metal and was only six inches high. It had been given by Mother Superior. The metal cross would outlast all of them.

When the grave was filled and topped, the nuns went back and prayed at the spot, then they got the wagon rolling toward Roswell.

The little sleep Spur had before dawn helped temper his fury at Clark. A judge and jury would be best, but there simply were no such niceties out here in the wilderness. He had talked with Mother Benedict and at last agreed to let Clark live until they came to the first civilized town, Roswell. There Clark would be turned over to the town lawmen and charged with murder. They would pause there for the trial.

Spur had insisted that Clark be tied in the wagon hand and foot, that he be untied only to relieve himself and Spur would oversee those short trips.

Clark glared at Spur, but had enough sense left not to roil the big man again.

All morning they plodded westward. Spur had been on cattle drives, where ten to twelve miles was a good day. But there you constantly had work to keep you busy. Here there was nothing to do but think and plan and let the dreary hours drag by.

After a half hour stop for a quick nooner, they moved on and Spur left Chiquita with the wagon and ranged ahead on his bay to check the lay of the land. They came to the spring they had searched for midway through the afternoon. It was still running and the water was pure and sweet.

It took them an hour to fill both of their barrels with water, then they moved again.

Chiquita took the lead, and less than a mile from the spring, Spur heard four rifle shots from ahead. He grabbed three loaded tubes of rounds for the Spencer and raced ahead.

Chiquita met him a quarter of a mile out.

"Two Mescaleros," she said. "They made sure that I saw them. It was a test, to see if the wagon people were armed and if they would fight."

"They know now."

She took a drink from her canteen. "They stood on the brow of a small ridge, skylining themselves so I couldn't miss them. I put two shots into the dirt in front of them, then two over their heads."

"They'll be back," Spur said.

"Yes, with plenty of help."

"How many?"

"The Mescaleros are scattered all over three states. They have trouble getting together for fiestas and celebrations, let alone for fighting. This would be a small loot affair. I would guess they would test us again with ten or twelve braves."

"Can we handle them?"

"If they all have rifles, we have a big problem."

They rode back to the wagon, told everyone what had happened, and got them ready. It was nearly four in the afternoon.

"They won't be back today," Chiquita said. "Mescaleros never fight at night, so we should be safe until tomorrow morning."

They stopped at five that afternoon in another shallow wash to get as far out of sight as possible. There was no advantage in secrecy now, Spur decided. He made each of the nuns shoot her rifle fourteen times, and change the loaded tube of rounds herself. His troops would not win any prizes for marksmanship, but they could throw out a lot of lead at anyone who attacked them.

Spur decided they would not unload the wagon to form a barricade to fight behind tonight. He wanted higher ground where he could at least see the enemy coming.

They moved before daylight, rolling through the pre-dawn darkness, into the scratchy light and then welcomed the sun's first full rays. Chiquita had directed the wagon along the spine of a low, rounded ridge. They could see five miles to the north and almost that far to the south.

Spur frowned and looked north again. The flash came again. The polished metal of a rifle receiver or un-blued barrel had glanced the sunlight his way. The Mescaleros were coming. Nobody had told them about sun flashes off rifles.

The nuns untied Clark and Spur made him help them unload a dozen heavy wooden boxes from the wagon and form them around the outside of the wheels. It created a miniature fort, with firing ports between the boxes. They had it high enough so it covered them when they sat down. They lined up the rifles around the square, and put loaded tubes of cartridges beside each weapon.

Chiquita and Spur took the watch. It was slightly after eight thirty when Chiquita spotted them.

"Four on my side, about three hundred yards out," Chiquita said.

"I can't see any to the south," Spur said. "Show me where the four are, the check this side." Spur found the hostiles, and the Breed looked the other direction.

"We'll let them get in to two hundred yards before we open fire," Spur said. "That means they have nothing to hide behind except sand out there."

Father Clark caught the Spencer Spur threw at him. He looked like he knew how to use a rifle.

"Shoot them out there, Clark, not us," McCoy said.

The priest nodded, hefted the rifle, then

sighted through the opening.

Sister Ruth had tears in her eyes. "I don't know if I can kill anybody!" she said.

"Sister Ruth, you just shoot high if you want to. The idea is to let them know we have a lot of rifles. Chiquita and I will try to cut down on their population."

"Now," Chiquita said. Spur leveled the Spencer repeating rifle through the niche between two boxes of Bibles and sighted in on a shadow in the sand where there should not be one. He fired, then watched the target. The round was a bit right. He corrected and fired twice and saw a sand colored form lift up, scream and fall to one side. Two rifles from the north fired at the wagon. Spur heard one round go through the canvas top, and another hit one of the wooden boxes and stopped.

Chiquita's rifle spoke twice behind him, Spur scanned the area and saw two more Mescaleros.

"You may fire now, ladies," Spur said. Three of you shoot to the front and three to the back. Let's do it."

He spotted another shadow on the open stretch nearly two hundred yards out and fired again. The shadow became a man who rolled to the left and out of sight into a small furrow.

Spur saw no more targets.

"Hold your fire to the north," he said. One more rifle was fired before the nuns stopped.

From the south a dozen rounds slammed into the boxes and the wagon. Spur felt the mules and horses were safe. The Mescals wanted the animals alive so they could ride or drive them back to their camp to use as food. A dead horse would have to be carried. Nobody carried a seven-dog.

"How many more?" Spur asked.

Chiquita fired and looked back. "One less. Four, maybe five. I've found two with rifles. One of them just went silent."

Spur moved to her side, spotted movement and put three bullets into the area as fast as he could lever new rounds into the Spencer. The movement stopped.

"Hold it," Spur said. The nuns on the south side stopped firing. "We may have discouraged them."

Chiquita agreed. "But they will be back. They need more braves, so one will run hard and fast to a neighboring camp or hunting area and bring them back. Six mules and five horses would feed their families for six months. This is not a prize they will give up as easily."

It was quiet then, deathly quiet as they waited. One of the nuns sat staring at the north, her lips moving without sound. Another sobbed behind one of the boxes.

Chiquita watched both sides for a few minutes, then crawled over to Spur.

"They're gone. Everyone has pulled back. That way we won't know where they are coming from next time. We should stay right here, no sense in trying to outrun them, it's too far."

Sister Teresa sat by the wheel loading tubes with cartridges for the rifles.

None of them had been hit. Father Clark sat beside the box staring to the north.

Chiquita took two extra tubes for her rifle and edged past one of the boxes.

"I'm going out there and check on the bodies. They left two dead they couldn't get to. I have to know if one of them is my brother—or my father. His name was Black Eagle, and he could still be an important chief with the Mescalero. I haven't heard anything about him since I came back this way."

"I'll come with you," Spur said.

She shook her head. "No, I go the Mescalero way. I don't want them to know I'm checking the bodies. I'll be back before you know it. I just have to be sure I didn't kill . . . That I didn't kill my brother, or my father."

FIFTEEN

The Indian was larger than most of the Mescaleros. He waved his rifle and the eight braves with him broke off the fight and faded into the rolling country to the north.

He glared at the braves and screeched at them.

"How could we fail? It was only one wagon. We are Mescaleros!" He stared at each brave until the man looked away. His name was Black Eagle, a subchief in the Mescalero tribes and leader of twenty families thirty miles to the north near a year round spring in a small green valley.

Hunting had been poor this year. Their lodges were empty, there was little food put away for the hard winter. The horses and mules that this roundeye party had would be enough to last them through the coldest year.

"We will not fail again. They are moving west. We will get to the place of the coyote and wait for them. Three of our braves will not be coming with us. We will wait for the wagon to move, then two of you will go back and help our brothers to their final resting place on the highest hill in the area, so their spirits may fly into the heavens.''

Black Eagle flexed his bronzed shoulders. There was a bullet wound on his upper arm. He bent, picked up a handful of sand and slowly poured it over the wound until it was filled. The bleeding stopped.

The subchief had a high forehead, black hair now showing traces of gray that had been tied in a loose twist down his back. His face was square and strong. The eagle is the king of the sky. So he must be as strong to lead his people. If he had not taken the Mexican woman into his lodge he would today be chief of all Mescaleros. She had shamed him, until he put her and her girl child out of his lodge and divorced them.

He wore only a loin cloth made of deer skin, and heavy moccasins worthy of long runs and hard battles. His lean, powerful body had a dozen scars on it from battles.

Black Eagle gave a curt hand signal and the small band of eight braves moved west. They had only three rifles. One had been lost in the attack. They would send a brave back to check for it when the wagon left, but chances are the roundeyes would look for it and take it with them.

This wagon was unusual. It was almost as if they were Mescaleros, or thought like Mescaleros. They protected themselves well and had many rifles. That was another big reason to capture this wagon. Six or seven more rifles from the roundeyes and many rounds of ammunition, would make Black Eagle the most feared subchief in the nation!

The raiding party had no horses. They walked or more likely trotted where they were going. They would set a pace that covered a mile in ten minutes, and they could maintain that rate for six hours without stopping. Such a six mile an hour pace was fifty percent faster than the usual four mile an hour that a horse or a mule traveled.

Most Mescalero braves could run forty miles and come up ready to fight.

The Mescalero raiding party with Black Eagle leading it, quickly outdistanced the plodding mules of the target wagon. Both headed west. Black Eagle moved steadily to his next attack point. This time he would pick the time and the place, he would have the advantage and surprise. He and his men would be victorious and win the horses and much more.

He could almost taste the sweet meat of the riding horses now after it roasted over an open fire!

Chiquita returned to the wagon after a twenty minute patrol. Spur gave her a drink and lifted his brows in question.

"We killed three of them, and they took one away. They'll be back for the others."

She handed Spur an old Sharps rifle.

"They are one rifle short, but will plan on getting it back. Knowing the Mescals, the leader has pulled his braves off and will attack us again where he wants to. They'll set up some sort of ambush and wait for us to walk into it."

"So we move on, now."

"Yes, and if we see anything that looks like it could foster a trap, we go around it, five miles out of our way if we have to. A detour is better than dead. The Mescalero is in no hurry. They know they have a hundred miles to jab at us, to look for an ambush spot, to find a weakness."

Spur pushed away from the shade of the wagon. The sun was still warm. He told the nuns it was time to pack up and move on. Even Clark helped, but quickly Spur tied him up inside the wagon, this time tied him to the big bell.

A half hour later the wagon was loaded. Spur showed the three riders how to tie a rifle onto the saddle, even though there was no rifle boot. He wanted them all to have a weapon close at hand.

Mother Benedict drove.

Spur moved out two hundred yards ahead of the wagon looking for problems, and Chiquita rode a half mile to three quarters of a mile ahead checking for any long range troubles and laying out a general route west.

Chiquita came back to Spur as it moved toward dusk.

"We better keep traveling," he said. "They won't attack us at night. We can drive until midnight, then take a break and look for a place to defend."

"That might not work, Spur. The Mescals are already ahead of us. The subchief or whoever leads the raid is looking for an ambush point. It won't help us to move by night." She nodded. "Believe me, Spur. I'm thinking like a Mescal raider. We can make only ten miles at night. The raiders can cover that distance in an hour and a half. They will know where we are. If we go 30 miles in 24 hours they can catch us in five hours of running."

"So there is no chance we can outdistance them?"

"Not unless we leave the wagon and everyone gets on horses and mules and we ride day and night."

"No chance."

"Let's drive until dark and make a quick camp. We're safe enough in the darkness."

Spur took the first watch as usual, and just after eleven o'clock he saw someone moving toward him from the blankets around the fire.

"Teresa, what are you doing out here?"

"Guess," she said. She wore the man's shirt that covered her to just below her waist. Now she opened it showing him she had on nothing under it. Her arms went around him and he felt her soft body pressed tightly against his.

"Teresa, we can't."

"We can. I'm not a nun, I never was a nun. I was forced into being a novice, remember?" She pushed one hand between their hips and found his crotch. A hard pole was already growing behind his fly. "You want to, I can tell."

"Oh, damn!"

"Right over here in moonlight. I'll spread out my shirt."

"You are terrible, Teresa!"

"And you love me being terrible." She reached up, put her arms around his neck and kissed him. "It gets lots better than that!" she whispered.

They sat on the ground, watched the stars for

a minute then she slipped out of the shirt.

"God, but you are beautiful in the moonlight!"

His hands moved to her breasts.

"You just like my breasts, my tits. You get all excited by tits, don't you?"

He bent and kissed them, then nibbled on the pink nipples. She waited for him to be satisfied there, then pushed him gently to his back and unbuttoned his fly.

"Tonight it's my party, I get to do what I want to." She opened his fly and reached inside. He had to help her get his erection free and jutting from his pants.

"I want to do you all the way, until you spurt it right in my mouth! I've been dreaming about this all week."

She moved lower until she hovered over his upright phallus, then dropped down on it. She pulled him into her mouth and then began to massage his scrotum.

"Oh, yes!" Spur said softly, then felt her head bobbing up and down on him and he moaned in delight.

Spur knew he couldn't hold out long. He caught her breasts with both hands and rubbed them.

She seemed to pull more of his big tool into her mouth and he felt it hit the back of her throat.

There was no way Spur could hold back then, the surges came and he tightened every muscle in his body as his hips jolted upward. Teresa made small sounds and stayed with him as he pumped six times and then relaxed.

A moment later she leaned over his face and kissed him and he kissed her back.

"That was great!" McCoy said.

"I hoped you would like it."

"Give me ten minutes and I'll repay the compliment."

They watched the stars. He stroked her breasts and they talked about what she would do when they got to Roswell.

"I'll go to the priest there, and explain it all, and ask him to release me from my vows because I'm not worthy. That's about the only thing that works."

He slid his hand between her legs and she laughed softly.

"First we have to get there. We have those Mescaleros out there somewhere."

"I don't want to worry about them. Right now is more fun, and what we're going to do. You rested up?"

"Insatiable, that's you. Never enough, you always want more."

"Depends on the man. I wouldn't let that priest touch my fingertips!"

"We agree on that." His hand moved upward until his fingers found a brushy jungle.

"Oh, yes, you're finding the way. Don't get lost."

He pushed her over on her back on her shirt and watched her in the moonlight.

"You are so beautiful, and so sexy, and so much fun to make love to. I hope you find a fine man who is rich and good to you. That probably won't be in Roswell, but it's a start."

He strummed her clit until she yelped and then climaxed in a flurry of tremors and contractions and spasms that turned her face into a mask of pleasure. When it passed she reached up and kissed him.

"Inside, now!"

He pushed into her and even when she put her legs around his back he found it took him longer to come to his own climax.

"You are getting tired," she said. "Teenage boys are remarkable. I saw one ejaculate six times once in an hour. It was a bet. He said I had to help, so I did. He just touched me. He was never inside me. That guy was amazing."

When Spur at last climaxed he finished it quickly and came away from her.

"I thought I heard something out there," he said sharply. He buttoned his pants and slid away into the night. Teresa put her shirt on and moved quietly back toward the wagon. He came to her before she got there.

"It was just a rabbit feeding," Spur said. "Damn good thing. A Mescal would have had both our scalps on his belt."

"They don't wear belts," Teresa said.

"You noticed."

He kissed her softly, pointed to her blankets and she hurried to them, waved and snuggled down to sleep.

Spur kept the rest of his rounds. The horses and mules were quiet, the big dipper swung around to the left making its circle around the North Star. He woke Chiquita at one A.M.

She came alert, put her knife away and glared at him.

"I hope you were satisfied."

"What do you mean?"

"Fucking that nun. How are you any better than Father Clark?"

"She came to me. Anyway, she isn't a nun. She hasn't taken her final vows. She's a novice. She's quitting the order as soon as we get to Roswell."

"Ha!"

Chiquita backed away from him. "Don't worry, I'll do my job. I was just surprised." She laughed quietly. "I guess I'll just have to prove to you I can do anything she can."

Chiquita grinned at him in the moonlight and faded into the darkness as she began making her rounds.

SIXTEEN

Everyone snapped and snarled the next morning, or it seemed that way to Spur. The whole group was on edge, nervous, worried. Mother Superior Benedict tried to calm everyone down, but it seemed only to make matters more touchy.

Breakfast was over quickly and they rolled. Spur had a talk with the Mother Superior about Clark. The man could shoot, they might need his trained hand. But he could also shoot Spur in the back and make a break for Roswell.

Spur decided to meet the problem head on. He untied the man from the big bell, let him rub out his wrists and then put him on one of the riding horses. Spur tossed him a Spencer, fully loaded and gave him three filled reload tubes.

"Clark. Way I figure it is a man has a right to defend himself against the Mescaleros. Your collar won't do a bit of good with them. If they take us, you'll be just another roundeye scalp on a lance drying in the sun."

Spur waited but Clark said nothing.

"Way I figure it too, is that you don't like me

none too well. The feeling is mutual. Problem is the Mescals hate both of us. When it comes down to the killing time, I'm counting on you shooting at the other guys, and not at me. Am I wrong?"

"You'll have to wait and see, won't you, McCoy," Clark said, a slow grin shading his face.

"Not by a damn sight, Clark! I get your word right here and right now, that you'll shoot that weapon only at the Mescals. You go back on your word I got five, six witnesses. They'll see that you are put away for good, whether I'm around or not. You read me true, whiskey priest?"

"Yes, yes. You have my word. Mother Benedict is all the witness you need. Where do you want me to patrol?"

"Hang on the south side of the wagon. They came from the north before. Figure the sneaky Mescals will hit us from the south this time. Stay close to the wagon. I'll be out front or slightly north. Mescals like to pull ambushes. I've seen them dig a hole and cover themselves with sand. Man can be six feet from them and never see them until they come up shooting. These savages are professional raiders, looters, warriors."

"I get the picture. I was a captain at Shenandoah, cavalry." He touched his fingers to his brow in a salute and rode twenty yards to the south of the wagon.

"You're a gambler, Mr. McCoy," Mother Benedict said. She bobbed her head, her face serious. "But this time I think it is a safe gamble. The man will try his hardest. He's been sober for two days now."

Spur swung up on his bay and rode. He went out a quarter of a mile and saw Chiquita on her roan gelding another half mile along the sweep of a gentle downgrade.

In the distance there were some breaks, a low bluff or ridgeline that was higher than anything for miles around. He studied it. The mass seemed to be ten, twelve miles long and at an angle across their route.

He rode forward until he caught Chiquita's attention, then she came to meet him.

She too had been looking at the bluff-like barrier.

"What do you think?" Spur asked.

"It's a long one, and it looks too steep to drive the wagon up and over. We go around it or find a way through it."

"Any water courses heading that way?" Spur asked.

She sent him a glance of appreciation. "You could be a scout yourself. Probably have been. A mile to the north there is what looks to be like a dent in the ridgeline. There could be a break there where these gushers boil through in the rainy season."

"Let's have a look," he said.

They both knew the wagon was safe. It was in the open with three riders around it, all with repeating rifles. And there was no good way to ambush it where it was.

They galloped a quarter of a mile, slowed to a gentle trot and soon came to a place where they could see that there plainly was a cut through

the bluff. A now dry water course meandered
across the high plateau's prairie and ended at
the sliced out section through the soft mound. It
had been no match for the raging waters that
finally broke through and then year by year kept
widening the cut.

The wagon was a mile and a half behind,
heading at the wrong angle for this new course.

"You go back and give Mother Superior our
new route," Spur said. "I want to check out that
gap. As you are thinking, that would be a great
spot to ambush a single wagon. Get everyone in
the gap and close both ends."

"Are you sure?"

"Yes. If I run into your Mescals, I'll hit them
with three quick shots so you'll know, then I'll
try to save my hide. They won't keep their
position if we know they are there."

"True. The Mescals are masters at running
away when outnumbered or outgunned to live to
fight another day." She smiled at him, pulled
her roan around and galloped toward the wagon.

Spur moved slowly toward his objective. It
was still four miles ahead. With luck the wagon
would get there about noon. He had over five
hours to do his recon. He rode out of sight of the
gap to the south, then masked behind the more
rolling plains, he came to within a quarter mile
of the cut still out of sight. Spur ground tied his
animal, then looped the reins around a low
growing, sturdy bush and slid the three tubes of
reloads for the Spencer inside his shirt. He
moved off like an Apache at a ground eating trot
toward the ridgeline.

He would come in from the other side of the

bluffs, work up to the top and see what he could see below. It took him another half hour to get into position. Then he edged to the top of the sandstone barrier and looked down into the other side, the approach the wagon would take.

Sand, rocks, the eroded sides of the cut which he saw now were almost fifty feet apart at the base where the dry water course angled through. Plenty of room for a wagon to get through. The water had created a smooth highway for them.

Sand, easy to dig, easy to cover up a Mescalero. He sectioned the sides of the approaches to the cut and stared at it in a yard by yard inspection. When he found nothing he took a new grid line, working across the approaches systematically so he would miss nothing.

When he had finished the horizonal grids, he fashioned vertical ones and checked the area again.

Nothing.

No depressions, no wagon wheel tracks. No straws sticking out of the sand. He snorted. He could see nothing that small from this distance. Would the Mescals bury themselves in place and wait five or six hours to spring their trap?

Absolutely!

He went down the reverse slope out of sight of anyone on the other side, then moved up to the lip of the cut and looked down into the water course between the smoothly worn sides.

No one there.

Again he worked his search grids, but could see nothing out of place.

They had to be here. It was the best ambush

position for ten miles any any direction. If he were an Apache he would certainly use it.

Rocks.

There were no big boulders or rocks anyone could hide behind. No jagged rock falls inside the cut or on the outside.

Strategy. They had no horses to they could not wait until the wagon was in the cut and then storm it from both ends. They had to be in place. He worked his way back to the lip of the ridge and nestled into the hot sand on the reverse slope. When he saw the wagon coming he could move up two feet and be in an ideal spot for supporting fire if it were needed. If the wagon rolled through without any ambush, he would borrow one of the horses and ride back and pick up his bay.

Wait. There was nothing to do but wait.

How did the Mescals do it? If they were down there covered with a layer of sand, it had to be twenty degrees hotter than Spur was.

The morning sun warmed, then became downright hot. Spur pushed up a foot and edged his head without hat over the ridgeline and looked to the east. He could see the top of the white wagon canvas rolling over the prairie. Another hour, maybe an hour and a half.

He had noticed some holes along the down slope of the bluff. Now he saw movement and eight feet down he spotted a triangular head slide out of a hole and deady eyes blink in the bright sun. The rattler paused for a moment, then slithered forward, and angled down the hill.

The snake was four feet long, with ten or

twelve rattle buttons on its tail. Spur watched it go, made sure it was moving well down the hill, then studied the other holes he could see. None were any closer to him. He divided his attention between the holes now, and the bobbing, rolling sight of the covered wagon.

The outriders had pulled in within twenty-five yards of the Conestoga. One rode on each side, and one behind. Chiquita was no more than fifty yards ahead of the mules.

They moved forward. The wagon was less than half a mile from the cut. Chiquita rode forward half that distance and looked at the cut, then at both sides and at the flared, level approach to the passage through the dry sand. To her nothing looked out of place. It didn't to Spur either and that was what bothered him the most.

The wagon rolled closer.

Of course! The ambushers would not be directly in the water course, they would be to the side of it so they would not be trampled by the mules! Again he studied the sides of the dry river. This area on both sides was not as smooth. It had lumps and some rock fall, but none larger than a bucket.

A chilling thought came to him. He had not checked out the far side of the top of the bluff! Across the fifty feet to the other half of the sandstone barrier there could be half a Mescalero tribe and he couldn't see them. Spur studied the slant of the sandstone again down the reverse slope. Evidently it dropped off lower because he could see only the front edge.

He laid out the three tubes of rounds, checked the Spencer again and eased up to the top of the ridge.

Chiquita sat on her horse twenty yards from where the wagon would hit the sand and move into the final approach to the cut. She was maybe fifty yards from the pass through the bluff. The wagon came slowly twenty yards behind her.

If it happened, they would wait for the wagon to be nearly to the mouth, then shoot a lead mule to stop it and pick off the surprised defenders.

Chiquita had kept the three outriders all behind the wagon now, back by fifty yards. Yes! The wagon could be all the way through before the last riders were even at the cut. Good strategy to spread out the people.

He watched silently as the wagon moved closer. Sweat dripped off his nose and his chin. He edged the blued barrel of the ten-pound .52 caliber rifle over the edge pointing down.

Nothing moved on the cliff or the slopes below. With six men on both sides of the cut he could hold off a company of infantry regulars.

Chiquita carried her rifle in one hand across her saddle. She stared at the slopes a moment, then spurred the gelding and it jolted foward. She rode hard into the start of the cut, then on through it.

Nothing happened.

Spur wiped sweat off his forehead before it got in his eyes. He scanned both sides of the route again. His side! If the Mescals were there they would be on his side with the braves on the ridge on the other side for crossfire! He scanned the slope below him.

It seemed to happen in frozen motion. Below as he watched, a patch of the sand and rocks erupted and a Mescalero brave lifted up, swinging his rifle to aim it toward Mother Superior.

Spur slammed the Spencer muzzle downward and blasted two shots so fast the Mescal never had a chance to fire. The Indian flopped back to the ground and never moved.

The moment the first shot sounded, Mother Benedict lashed at the mules with the long reins, screaming at them, slapping them to move forward faster.

Two more Mescals near the first one lifted from the sand below and fired, but their shots were hurried. The first clipped Mother Superior's right arm, the second went through the top of the wagon. Spur shot one of the Indians through the head, brought his rifle around to bear on the other one when a shot from the mouth of the cut hit the brave, knocking him backwards into the dust.

One more enemy rifle blasted from the top of the cliff across the way. Spur moved his sights that way and saw three Mescaleros standing on the ridge line. A shot from behind the wagon cut down the brave with the rifle, and the other two released arrows, then dropped out of sight.

The mules had responded slowly to the whipping, but now surged ahead into a trot, and slanted the Conestoga into the cut and out of sight. Spur put three more rounds over the ridge line across from him to discourage any more arrows from that quarter. Below he saw the three horseback riders come into the cut and through it at a gallop.

Father Clark brought up the rear pounding off shots as he rode aimed at the cliff top where the Indians had been.

Spur looked below. Three Mescals lay where they had fallen. The rifles were more important than the braves now. McCoy slid over the top of the ridge and scrambled down the other side. An arrow slapped the rocks just behind him. He turned and sent two rounds at the ridge line, then he was down.

He caught up the first rifle, pryed the second one from dead fingers and fired a round point blank into the third Mescalero who suddenly came alive, and reached for his rifle. The Indian slammed backward into the ground as half the top of his skull blasted into the reddish stone, turning it pure red.

Spur carried the three weapons like cord wood as he jogged to the south toward his horse. He was soon out of arrow range but there was still a rifle on the far cliff.

He saw a rifle bullet plow up dirt in front of him and then heard the sound of the shot. They did not have repeaters. He ran again, angled lower on the side of the bluff and then into the flatness of the rolling plain. One more shot came, but it was not a marksman behind the weapon.

Spur hurried with his forty pounds of rifles, and ten minutes later found his bay mare where he had left her. He mounted, put two rifles in the boot and carried one over each shoulder by the slings, then rode straight for the bluff. It was not so high nor steep that a good horse could not walk up it.

His bay made the job look easy, and a half hour later he caught up with the wagon where it had stopped a mile from the cut, and a mile from the Mescaleros.

Teresa had bound up Mother Superior's arm.

"The bullet went all the way through, Mr. McCoy. Don't look so worried," Mother Benedict said. "I was the only casualty. Chiquita thinks we were lucky, and that you were in exactly the right place."

Chiquita came up and suggested they move on. They did. Spur found out that Father Clark had been the one to cut down the rifleman on the ridge.

"Old habits die hard, Captain," Spur told him.

Father Clark looked up and nodded. "Sometimes they don't die at all. All of the soldiering." He turned away and then rode back, handed Spur the rifle and two reload tubes. "You better keep these." He wheeled the horse and moved to his position behind the wagon as rear guard.

Spur and Chiquita rode a hundred yards ahead of the Conestoga.

"How did you know where they would be?" she asked.

"Basic military science," Spur said. She looked up puzzled.

"I just tried to think what I would do, how I would trap the enemy in the same place. I figured it out almost too late."

"But not really too late. They should have had us dead. You saved all of us."

"Our equipment saved us. If they had put six repeating rifles on both sides of the cut, we all would be dead."

"Whichever way, I'll take it," she said. "They will try again. Even though they may only have one rifle now. They have lost six braves. They will come at us with more men and more rifles the next time. We should have two days before they can get a force to hit us."

"That puts us two days closer to Roswell, but still about three days away," Spur said.

SEVENTEEN

As Chiquita predicted, the next two days on the trail went well and without any attacks by the Mescaleros. The route slanted slightly north to compensate for their south swing, and angled for Roswell. Spur had no idea how far away they were now. Chiquita said on the second day after the Indian attack that there were two, perhaps three good days of riding yet before they saw Roswell.

Little Blossom was thriving on her combination of soup and sugar water. She needed milk, but another few days would not harm her growth. The nuns fussed over Blossom like she was a choice toy, a favored duty. She would be spoiled totally within three months, Spur decided.

The third day after the attack began as the others, a quick breakfast of the last of the bacon, some hardtack mixed in and then biscuits and coffee.

They were on the trail shortly after sunup. Spur rode up to Father Clark, who had asked to ride rear guard. The Secret Service agent looked at the whiskey priest. He was still sober.

Spur handed him a Spencer barrel first.

"You should have one of these. Chiquita says the Indians could be back for a visit today or tomorrow."

Father Clark held the barrel of the Spencer. "You think you can trust me?"

"Have so far. You can use that rifle, that's the important thing. You don't want to be scalped anymore than I do. You know I also can use a rifle, so why cut down your odds of getting killed by the hostiles by blowing my head off? You're an intelligent man, Clark. So am I, Harvard class of fifty-eight. Let's just say we have an armed truce until we get out of here. Then if you want to play a game of hide and seek in the desert with me, with the Spencers as referee, I'll play."

Clark grinned. "I'm not that dumb, McCoy. I've seen you shoot. I'll go with the detail and take my chances when we get to Roswell. Oh, I thought about charging off when we're a day away. Figured you'd come hell-bent and ventilate my hide with about seven rounds from your Spencer. I play the odds. If we get through, I'll keep on playing them. Right now the odds are stay with the detail and throw out lots of lead."

Spur pushed his hat back and lit a thin, black, twisted cheroot as he stared at Clark. "You were probably a damn good soldier, Clark. Don't see where you went wrong."

He reined the bay around. "Keep a sharp lookout to the rear. Remember they will be running, and the little bastards can't hide when they're jogging along." He kicked the bay and rode to the front, then on to where Chiquita rode the point.

There was no real trail. Here and there they saw wagon tracks, but the country was so open that one line across the prairie was as good as the next. West was the direction, and now slightly north of west to bring up Roswell.

Here and there they found grass on the rocky barren soil. A few sparse shrubs and sages grew in patches. He saw Chiquita stop and then ride to her left, due south. She went fifty yards, then swung down from her mount.

Spur charged that way at a gallop.

When he got there, he found Chiquita giving a whiskered old man a drink of water. He had the look of a prospector, but there was no gold out here.

Spur dismounted. The man sat in a small depression and had been trying to get a fire going. He had used the last of his matches without success. There was no mule or donkey. He had only a dirty pillowcase near where he had stopped.

The man was almost dead from heat prostration and exposure. They wet his lips with water. He licked them. They let him suck on a wet cloth for five minutes, then gave him a small sip of water. When he could talk he touched Chiquita's hand.

"Thanks," he said slowly. His tongue still swollen.

"I'll get the wagon over here," Spur said.

A half hour later the oldtimer was in the back

of the wagon. Sister Ruth let him sip water slowly. He was sunburned and had lost a lot of water from his body. Gradually Spur got his story. He had been prospecting, then his mule died after drinking some bad water, and he ran out of food.

"Would have been all right if I'd stayed with the mule. Could have eaten off her for two days before she went rancid. But I figured I could walk all night and be nigh on to Roswell by morning. Turned out I was wrong. You say we're still more than two days from that little town?"

Spur left him talking with the nuns and went back to the point. Chiquita had seen no evidence of the Mescaleros.

"We won't walk into an ambush spot this time," she said. "There seems to be nothing out here but plains."

"So what is their strategy to handle this terrain?" Spur asked.

"They will hit us while we're moving. So we don't have time to set up a barricade like we did last time. For this attack they will have more rifles, more men."

"Then to counter them we turn the inside of the wagon into our fort. We put the boxes around the sides and cut holes in the canvas to shoot through." He pulled his mount around. "I'll get busy on that, you be careful."

He rode hard back to the wagon and began moving boxes, putting the wooden ones on their sides and cutting firing slots in the heavy canvas.

The old prospector's name was Edgar. He watched the procedure for a few minutes.

"I take it, young feller, that we're looking to be visited by the Mescals."

"They'll be back, they owe us, and they want our horses and mules for food."

"Figures. Got an extra Spencer like I seen around here?"

Spur gave him one and put him to refilling empty reload tubes.

"Handy dandy little gun," Edgar said. "This the one the Rebels said the Yankees loaded in the morning and fired all day."

Spur kept working. A half hour later he had room for four people inside the wagon fully protected behind the boxes. Each had a firing slot to shoot from and a foot square hole in the canvas to see through.

Edgar approved and took over one of the firing slots.

"Bring on them damn Apaches!" Edgar said. "Been wanting to even up with them ever since they got away with my mule and my traveling kit last year. Only thing they didn't get was my scalp."

Spur checked the outriders. None had seen anything. Teresa was on a horse just behind the wagon. He rode knee to knee with her a moment.

"The other night was delicious, you ready to try me again?" she asked.

"First the redskins, then the pretty, naked lady. But in Roswell. Too damn dangerous out here right now to take our clothes off." He left her grinning and rode back to see Chiquita.

Just before noon the Mescaleros attacked. Ten of them had been hiding behind small bushes and in the sand to the north. They lifted up and fired four rifles and bows and arrows in a sudden move that caught the travelers by surprise.

"Into the wagon!" Spur bellowed. Already he heard return fire. Father Clark had seen the start and from his drag spot had begun firing almost at once. Chiquita rode back from her place three hundred yards ahead of the wagon. Before she got to the wagon, another ten braves rose up to the south and began firing.

Sister Maria had been riding flanker to the south. The first volley from three more rifles blew Maria from her saddle. Her horse reared, then raced away from the shots.

Spur had talked with Mother Benedict and Sister Ruth the other driver about this situation. The plan was to whip the mules and run forward as quickly as possible. This would make the Indians move as the wagon rolled, get them out of their hiding places.

Now Mother Benedict lashed the reins at the mules who walked faster, but would not break into a trot.

It didn't matter. A moment later two rifle bullets slammed into the lead right mule's head and it went down in the traces, dead in ten seconds and the wagon came to a halt.

Spur leaned behind his bay and fired over her back as he raced for the wagon. He fired at the braves on the south side. There was no chance to try to get Sister Maria. He felt a rifle round slice over his head, and ducked lower. A moment later he was at the wagon and he tied his bay there, then squirmed behind a wheel and began firing at the brown on brown patches in front of him to the south. He saw one brave move, and Spur sighted in and squeezed off the round.

The big Spencer round dug into the Mescalero and tore through his heart, dumping him into his happy hunting ground forever. Fire from the wagon came rapidly now. Spur could tell that all four of the firing slots were in use. Clark had gone down behind his horse somewhere to the rear, and soon his Spencer spoke with authority.

The first of the Mescalero barrage was over. Spur guessed they were short on rifle rounds. He saw them begin to creep forward through the uneven ground and sparse vegetation. McCoy tracked one Indian moving forward, sighted in and the next time the Indian slithered forward on his stomach, Spur put a round through the top of his head.

Two down.

Mother Benedict had leaned into the wagon when the mule went down, caught up her Spencer and got to a firing position. She was not thinking of her vows or of the church, she was simply trying to stay alive. She fired at the brown shapes fifty to sixty yards ahead of her to the north. They moved silently forward. She fired again and again. She reloaded the tube and fired at the forms. At last she hit one. She didn't weep, she wasn't sorry for the savage. He was trying to kill her! She went on firing with a renewed vengeance.

Teresa had seen the first attack and rode to the wagon safely. She was inside reloading tubes with shells and trying to keep Blossom from crying.

Chiquita saw quickly that she could never get

to the wagon. She swung to the side and to the rear of the hostiles on the south. She got down from her mount, tied him to a sage and took the three tubes of shells and worked silently forward. A small hummock only six feet above the plain, gave her an observation point.

She saw the Mescaleros now in front of her and only seventy-five yards away. They had closed to fifty yards of the wagon. She lay down, cleared some grass so she had a perfect field of fire, and sighted in on the first Mescalero. She fired, moved to the second one and fired. By the time her seven shot tube of rounds was empty, three of the Mescals were dead or wounded so seriously they couldn't fight. Two of the Indians raced toward her. She slid in a second tube and brought down one of them at thirty yards and the other dove into the sand and rolled away.

On the far side, Father Clark had the same idea. He was outside the attack zone, and swung to the north where he saw the savages. He counted twelve, then sat on his horse and fired seven rounds at them, killing at least one. The others turned, spotted him and four of them moved toward him.

He rode straight at them, firing as he went. He killed three before one of their rifle rounds caught him in the shoulder and blasted him from the saddle. He grabbed his two full tubes of shells and rolled behind a rock. The hostiles were out there somewhere. He would take as many of them with him as he could!

Besides that, he could put a large hole in their trap. If he managed to blast enough of the hostiles up here, Spur could cut that dead mule out of the traces and get the wagon moving. Yes! He had to do that.

He felt his shoulder and his hand came away bloody. But he could still lift his left arm. It couldn't be that bad. He would make the bastards pay!

A Mescalero lunged at him from nowhere. Clark's Spencer came up with precision as he triggered the weapon, the round splashing through the redskin's throat, changing his flight path and dumping him into the stones and dirt six feet away.

There would be more. He lifted up and fired four times at the Mescaleros shooting at the wagon. One screamed and rolled over. Two more dodged back from their vantage point to take cover.

"Now!" he screamed toward the wagon. "Get that wagon out of here!"

Clark was not sure if anyone heard him. He would call again, each time he had a chance. It could work. For a moment he thought of the line from Charles Dickens, "It is a far, far better thing I do, then I have ever . . ." Two Mescaleros interrupted him. He shot one, slammed the butt of the Spencer into the skull of the second, killing him.

Father Clark chuckled softly to himself and aimed the long Spencer at the savages out there trying to kill his friends.

"Get that wagon out of here now!" he screamed again.

Under the wagon, Spur McCoy heard the words. Clark was right. If they stayed there the hostiles could pick them off one by one. The level of firing had slowed from the south where Clark was. Spur drew his four-inch hunting knife that was sharp enough to shave with and worked his way slowly under the wagon to the front, then under the tongue and between the stamping mules.

He should be able to get to the traces and the harness connectors and cut the dead animal free. If the Mescals saw him he would be a new target.

Spur moved slowly, hoping not to attract the enemy's notice. One mule saw him and stomped to the side as far as the harness would let it move. Spur talked to them, chattered with the three skitterish animals, trying to calm them.

After five minutes he was at the dead animal. He slashed the leather straps, cut them cleanly and unhitched the straps on the doubletree. Just two more leathers and they could leave.

He lunged forward, sliced the last of the harness, stood and ran around the lead mule and back to the wagon wheel. Spur leaped on the seat, whacked the mules with the reins and got them moving.

"Let's get out of here!" Spur bellowed. "Keep firing as long as you can see them. They'll be running after us."

Mother Benedict leaned out from the covered section and reached for the reins. Spur vaulted off the slowly moving rig, found his bay walking along behind the wagon and shouted for everyone to move out.

Edgar looked out the end of the wagon at Spur as he mounted, ducking a rifle round. Spur rode up to the wagon and waved at Edgar.

"Hey, we running away from the fun? I was just getting my shooting eye back."

"Shoot all you want to, Edgar, they'll be coming after us for several miles."

Spur turned and looked where Sister Maria lay. There was no chance to go back for her, not even to see if she were alive or dead. But he knew she was dead by the way she lay, sprawled with her head to one side at an unnatural angle. Spur sent a pair of shots at the Indians, and kicked the bay into a gallop heading west.

EIGHTEEN

Sporadic gunfire followed the wagon as it bounced and rattled along at more than its normal speed. Spur and Chiquita rode the rear guard, firing whenever they saw a Mescal run close enough so they could get a good shot at him.

Gradually the wagon and the horses tired out the running Indians and they fell behind.

The Breed rode up beside Spur as they checked their back trail again.

"You know why we got out of their trap, don't you, McCoy?"

"Yes. Because of what Father Clark did."

"Yes. He rode directly into their north side ambushers. I saw him riding and firing until he was knocked off his horse."

"He kept them busy enough so we had time to cut the mule free and get moving out of the trap."

"The church will make a hero of him," Chiquita said. She lifted the Spencer and sent two shots into a brown smear at the side of a small bush three hundred years away that could have been a Mescalero.

They turned and rode hard for two hundred yards, then paused and looked to the rear again.

"It was Father Clark's final atonement. He knew he was in the worst trouble of his life."

Spur agreed with a nod. "I said he would die for his sins, and he sure did. I didn't think he would pick the time and the place for it to happen."

"What about Sister Maria?" Chiquita asked.

"Dead. No other answer. She was killed instantly when they shot her in that opening volley. I saw the way she fell. Her neck was broken as well. Anyway, now that we've left the area . . ." He did not continue.

"I better tell Mother Benedict," Spur said at last. He rode ahead to the wagon, suggested they slow the mules to normal speed and then he told Mother Benedict about Sister Maria and what happened.

The sturdy nun listened to his description of how the sister died.

"We knew she was not here, but we hoped that somehow . . ." Mother Benedict wiped a tear away. "There is no chance for a Christian burial, for the last rites . . . Oh. Father Clark, too." Her face contorted and she turned away. "Dear Lord in Heaven, that is three of our party!"

"Mother Benedict, we're going to make damn sure that there are no more killed on this trip." Spur wheeled rode to the back of the wagon.

"Edgar!" he called.

The old prospector wormed out from between

the boxes.

"Yes sir, you called?"

"Ever driven a team of four . . . well, three now."

"Does the Big Dipper swing around the North Star? Course I have. Suggest we take that other lead mule off. Won't do no good, cause nothing but trouble."

"Good, Edgar. You take over the driving chores."

Back up front, Spur told Mother Benedict he wanted her to be with the remaining nuns. No one else would ride horses. She had four nuns left out of six. They left the boxes the way they were inside the wagon for protection. Mother Benedict had to tell the others about Father Clark and Sister Maria.

Spur helped unhitch the third mule and roped her behind the other two on a lead line.

The wagon rolled along.

McCoy rode up to Chiquita and asked her to pull back within a hundred yards of the wagon.

"I'm going to swing down our back trail a ways and see how our Mescal friends are doing. Will they keep following us now? We hurt them badly?"

"Depends how hungry they are. My guess is that they will give it up and go back to their lodges. They are not used to losing so many men on a raid. Especially one that produces nothing but widows. But, you be careful back there."

Spur touched his hat brim and rode. He had three full tubes of rounds for the Spencer. That gave him twenty-eight shots. He drifted a quarter of a mile to the left as he worked back the trail. Every quarter mile he paused and studied the terrain. There was no way that even a Mescalero could hide as he jogged forward. Spur checked the land for a mile across, but could see no movement.

Once he thought he had a Mescal, but it turned out to be a coyote running from one small bush to the next as it worked away from the hated man smell.

When he was about three miles back, Spur turned and rode toward the wagon. The Mescals had turned back, or were circling them wide to hit them once more. Spur McCoy did not know which.

The last attack had come about ten in the morning. Spur looked up at the sun and saw that it was nearing three in the afternoon. They had missed their noon break.

By the time Spur rode back to the wagon, Mother Benedict was driving again, with her bandaged arm showing some signs of bleeding. Edgar rode the one saddle horse they had left. He met Spur a hundred yards out.

"Troops are wondering about a rest. We need to change the mules too. Have to do it every half day with just two to pull."

"Do it," Spur said. "Stop it anywhere. I'll go get Chiquita."

Sister Ruth gave them strips of jerky to chew on and dried fruit for their meal. She made coffee. It was a somber group. The four nuns clustered together. Spur and Sister Cecilia unhitched the mules and rotated two fresh ones into the traces.

They had stopped less than half an hour when

everyone was back on the wagon ready to go.

Edgar slid into the driver's seat and they rolled.

The country they passed was much the same as it had been, high and dry, a plateau that stretched for what looked like a thousand miles Westward.

Spur made one more two mile circle to the rear, but raised no Mescal fire and saw no movement. He was not convinced that the raiders had given up yet. They had one dead mule and two horses if they could catch them. That might be enough to show for their work and their losses.

They camped the night in a small depression that could almost qualify as a valley. The water course through it was dry, and there was no water anywhere.

Chiquita said this was new territory to her. The Mescals she moved with never came this close to Roswell when she was with them. There could be more water during the next day and a half to two days and there might not be. She decided they should go on short water rations just to be sure.

Water could be used only for cooking, drinking, and a small drink for the animals.

Edgar shook his head when they asked him about water. He couldn't remember even coming through this part of the country, but he must have.

"Consarn it, ladies, this just beats the consarnits out of me! Wish I could be more help."

Spur stood the first watch as usual, and was

joined by Edgar.

"Consarn it, looks like I should be helping a little. You folks saved my old worthless hide, that's for consarn sure!"

They talked softly, listened and watched.

"Them Mescals is twenty miles the other way by now," Edgar said. "They got themselves one dead mule to butcher and cut up, and two scalps, and two live horses to haul the meat on. Land sakes, they probably were butchering that mule five minutes after we hightailed out of there. Then they sent two or three of their braves chasing us just to get rid of us. Course they'll hide out somewhere and cook the liver and brains most likely."

"I really hope that you're right, Edgar. But I'm not counting anything for sure until we're safe and sound inside some hotel in Roswell."

They woke Chiquita at two and she scolded them, but she had appreciated the extra two hours of sleep. "Now you two get some sleep," she said.

Spur slept little thinking about the three who had died in the trip. He had warned them, but still it riled him that they had been lost when he was leading the escort. At last he rolled over and went to sleep.

Chiquita's toe nudged him awake. It was daylight. They were almost packed and ready to go.

"You're not the only one who can let a person get some extra rest," she said. She sat down beside him with a tin plate of fried potatoes and onions with the last strips of bacon and fresh biscuits for him. The coffee was scalding hot, black and there was plenty left.

The wagon rolled at six A.M.

Chiquita rode to the front to scout the trail.

Spur rode to the rear to check out the back trail in one long loop.

Edgar rode beside the wagon trying to watch all four ways at once.

Edgar and Chiquita decided the Mescals were well on their way back to their lodges, but Spur was not so sure. He held out for vigilance, and made two three-mile loops on their back trail before noon.

They cut a small river about eleven in the morning, and paused to let all of the stock drink their fill. Upstream they found a good place and refilled their water barrels. The women washed their faces and arms and waded in the cool water and splashed, enjoying the relief from the perpetual heat. They sounded like excited, happy children.

If anything it was hotter now than it had been the past ten or eleven days. Everyone had lost track of how long they had been on the trail.

They had cooked oatmeal for their noon dinner. It had been peppered with cut up pieces of dried fruit that soaked up and became delicious as they cooked. There was no milk, but plenty of sugar, and Ruth had made sure the oatmeal was a little watery.

A new feeling swept through the eight adult travelers. It was a sense that they were going to make it. They had decided that the worst was over and they could walk on into Roswell now if they had to!

Edgar shouted an hour after they rolled, and pointed to the west.

"Dadblamed bluff over there! Remember seeing that the first day on my ride out. We can't be much over a day from Roswell! Know that danged bluff anywhere!"

Chiquita heard him and rode toward it. She came back two hours later. She had ridden to the top of it and through a light haze had seen green splotches ahead and what looked like about a hundred cooking stove smokes. There could be only one answer to the question.

"It must be Roswell out there about ten miles!" she said.

Everyone cheered. Two of the sisters started to cry and Spur McCoy heaved a small sigh. But he was not going to let down his guard just yet.

They camped that night in the shadow of the big bluff, found another small stream and Mother Superior and the nuns all had quick baths in the cool water.

That night when Spur woke Chiquita at twelve o'clock, she touched his arm.

"Wait a minute," she said. She reached up and kissed him. "I want you to know that if I had a mind to, I could show you all sorts of interesting Indian ways to make love. But right now is not the time. We have to get what's left of our charges safely into Roswell. Perhaps you'll have a hotel room, and I will come visit you."

She slid away from him without waiting for a reply. Spur smiled and waved at her in the dark, then found his blanket and tried to go to sleep.

Tomorrow, Roswell, New Mexico Territory!

NINETEEN

The wagon arrived in Roswell the next afternoon just before three in the afternoon. They drove straight to the small Catholic church and Mother Superior Benedict took charge. She had the nuns all dressed in their regular habits and once again they did look like nuns.

She paid Chiquita the agreed to fee and suggested that she keep one of the Spencer rifles as well. They shook hands and the small guide rode her horse back toward Main street.

Spur shook hands with the five ladies and rode away, heading for the livery stable, then a hotel and a long hot bath and all the thick steaks he could eat.

The nuns would remain at the church until they had new orders from their bishop. They would need a new priest and replacement nuns for those lost. It was the end of their journey for a few months at least.

Edgar had dropped off the wagon when they passed the first saloon. He said he still had a few dollars and his credit was good all over town.

Spur found the sheriff's office and reported the deaths of the three citizens on the trail all attributed to Mescalero raiding attempts.

The sheriff was a short, fat man who did not wear a gun. He lit a cigar and snorted.

"Damn lucky to get through, I'd say. The Mescals have been raising all kinds of hell out this way. Army cut off any more escorts as I guess you found out. Well, I'll record the deaths for the books. A Catholic priest and two nuns, you said? Sounds like a risky trip. You have a scout?"

"Chiquita, a Mescal Breed."

The sheriff grinned. "No damn wonder you made it through. That little lady thinks Mescal out there. No damn wonder. She's the best scout in half a dozen states."

"What about mail. Any going through to Denver?"

"Not out of here. We might get something over toward Phoenix and maybe Sante Fe if the stage ever gets back to running. You in a rush to send a letter?"

Spur grinned. "Not really. What's the best hotel in town, one with a bathtub and lots of hot water?"

The man said the Westerner, and Spur walked out, stretched and then wandered around until he found the hotel.

He finished his bath in the special room at the end of the second floor of the hotel and went back to his room wearing a robe and carrying his thick towel. The door to his room was open a thin crack. His guns were inside. He tried to look inside, but he could see nothing. Someone with coffee and asked what was for desert.

Three hours later they sat in the hotel dining room. Spur had a two pound T-bone steak with four vegetables, a cold beer, a quart mug filled

"You just got yourself a guide."

Chiquita giggled.

"I want to unbraid that long black hair and help you have another bath. I go crazy in a bath-tub."

"Yeah, roundeye?"

"One request," he said, slipping out of the robe.

"Not lately."

"Anyone ever tell you that you look a little like an Indian?"

Spur bent and kissed her gently pouting lips.

"We've got the rest of the afternoon, and then dinner in that fancy dining room downstairs, and then all night. If you're disappointed after that, Mr. McCoy. I guarantee I'll do it again and again and again, until I can satisfy you."

"I'm used to the best guides in the West. I wouldn't want to be disappointed."

Spur dropped his towel and key and walked over to the bed and sat in front of her.

"Hey, stranger. You looking for a good guide? One that knows the territory and how to get from one place to the other? I could even show you where the bed is."

Chiquita sat on the bed. She had taken off her tan shirt and now lowered her arms and lifted her chest and smiled at him.

started up the steps and he moved quickly, stepping inside and closing the door.

SAVAGE SISTERS

Briefly he thought of Major General Wilton D. Halleck back there in Washington, D.C. He would be waiting to hear. But from Roswell, New Mexico Territory the mail might not go out for a week or more, maybe two weeks.

He had time. First he had to rest up, and get his strength back with some good food, taste a bit of fine brandy and some of the local whiskey. Naturally he had to stock up on his supply of thin, black cheroots.

He would send off a letter tomorrow or the next day, or the next. Chiquita would get bored with town life after maybe only a week. Then he would figure out how he was going to get back to civilization. Santa Fe probably, and then a stage coach ride or a horse to Sand Creek and Fort Wallace in Missouri. He could catch a train there and send a telegram.

"Dessert's here," Chiquita said.

Spur looked down. She had ordered a whole lemon cream custard pie with egg white frosting.

Spur McCoy knew he was going to die, but what better way than eating yourself into a stupor?

He had his first bite then glanced up and saw a beautiful girl come into the dining room looking around. She saw him and her face brightened.

The girl was Teresa, in civilian dress. She was not a nun anymore and she walked straight for his table. It was going to be one hell of a week!